He wanted Francesca...

Tony leaned his forehead against the elevator wall, reliving the surprised look on her face when he'd nearly kissed her in the kitchen earlier. What in the world was wrong with him? Thankfully, the doors opened, saving him from reliving that exciting, *wonderful,* awful moment. Again.

Eyes half-closed, he stumbled to his room, only to curse when he reached into his pocket and found it keyless. He leaned back against his door. Maybe he could just sleep in the hallway. He didn't want to wake anybody up, least of all Francesca, though she was in the room right next door. The sight of her mussed and sleepy eyed would overload his already weak system.

But then a part of his still-functioning brain—and where was *that* earlier when he'd been gazing at his best friend as if she was a steak and he a vegetarian who'd fallen off the wagon—reminded him about the key code.

He opened one eye long enough to input his code— the day he and Francesca had met in the fourth grade—and opened the door with a sigh of relief.

In the dark, Tony toed off his shoes, then stripped off his clothes. Little did he know he wasn't alone....

Dear Reader,

The idea behind this story wasn't a hard one to come up with—I've always wanted to do a story about best friends falling in love. There's something about the level of intimacy already established, the *history* between close friends that makes falling in love more difficult—and in the end, so much more satisfying....

But if my smart, successful heroine was going to fall in love and risk nearly twenty years of friendship, the hero had to be irresistible. So what kind of man could be a more perfect match for her than a rich, gorgeous Italian charmer? Maybe he's got a few commitment issues, and his list of conquests is organized by zip code, but, hey, that's just Tony.

I'm willing to bet, though, that you'll thoroughly enjoy watching my heroine, Francesca, tame him....

I love to hear from readers! Visit my Web site at www.wendyetherington.com or write me via regular mail at P. O. Box 3016, Irmo, SC 29063.

Enjoy!

Wendy Etherington

Books by Wendy Etherington

HARLEQUIN TEMPTATION
944—PRIVATE LIES

WENDY ETHERINGTON

ARE YOU LONESOME TONIGHT?

This Book Belongs To:

Stephinslo

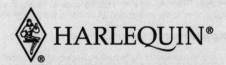

HARLEQUIN®

TORONTO • NEW YORK • LONDON
AMSTERDAM • PARIS • SYDNEY • HAMBURG
STOCKHOLM • ATHENS • TOKYO • MILAN • MADRID
PRAGUE • WARSAW • BUDAPEST • AUCKLAND

To Jacquie D'Alessandro and Jenni Grizzle,
who constantly, through every book, scene and sentence
remind me that I can do this.

And thanks to my editor, Brenda Chin,
for always steering me right.

ISBN 0-373-69158-0

ARE YOU LONESOME TONIGHT?

Copyright © 2004 by Wendy Etherington.

Printed in U.S.A.

1

"CHES, hand me a power cord."

Francesca D'Arcy eyed the jeans-clad lower half of her best friend and business partner, Anthony Galini. Not a bad way to start a Tuesday morning, truth be told. The man did have an amazing body, and he was presently defenselessly flat on his back beneath his desk.

She could envision dropping beside him, pulling his snug black T-shirt from his jeans, rolling up the soft cotton to reveal the sprinkling of jet-black hair against his olive-toned skin, his washboard abs, his broad chest—

Tony nudged her with his bare foot. "Ches!"

"What? Oh, the cord." She rummaged through the box of computer supplies sitting on the desk. "Uh— which one would be the power cord?"

"The one with three prongs that you'd plug into the wall," Tony said dryly.

"Cooking's my forte, not computers," she muttered, yanking out cord after cord in search of the proper one.

"*Somebody* got up on the wrong side of the bed this morning."

"At least I got *in* bed before this morning."

It seemed even Tony's commitment to the resort and winery they were about to open together couldn't compete with his goal of dating every gorgeous blonde in New York before he turned thirty. She'd lain awake until two-fifteen this morning—when she'd heard Tony enter his room at the resort, the one right next to hers.

"Which svelte blonde was it this time? Bambi? Or maybe it was Bunny?"

"I'll have you know I've never gone out with anyone named Bambi or Bunny." He paused. "But if you want to introduce me..."

As she finally pulled the right cord out of the box, she dropped it on him. Well, more accurately, she threw it on him.

"Ow! What is *with* you today?"

It was ridiculous, she knew, but her resentment at being relegated to "good ole dependable Ches" was especially sharp this morning. She hadn't realized her proximity to Tony over the last several months would bring her semi-dormant lust for him roaring to the surface. Lust she planned to do nothing about, of course. With a friendship that had begun in Mrs. Galloway's fourth-grade class, she'd had nearly twenty years to tell him about her attraction, and now, in the most important month of their lives, when the professional and personal pressure was the greatest, she was going to attempt to jump his bones?

Think again, sister.

Think business. All business.

She'd sunk every spare penny she had in Bella Luna, the newest brainchild of Tony's uncle Joe, the patriarch of the Galini family. The Galinis had tended to grapevines in Europe for over a hundred years, and fifteen years ago Joe had bought the eighty acres here on the North Fork of Long Island and built a successful winery in America. With all the new resorts and spas popping up in the area, Joe had recently decided to jump into a new venture and build his own resort. Unfortunately for Joe, two of his own sons were busy running the vineyard in Italy, and most of Tony's other cousins were fairly worthless in the ambition department. They were all content living off their trust funds, playing tennis at their country clubs, skiing in the Alps, and clubbing in New York.

In truth, Tony had spent a good many years indulging in the same pursuits. Then suddenly, six months ago, he'd called Francesca and asked her if she wanted to run the resort. With construction already underway, he'd sent her building and business plans, estimated costs and profit potential. With her degree in hotel and restaurant management, as well as certification from culinary school, Francesca had been completely unfulfilled working in convention planning at the New York Hilton, and after seeing Tony's ideas for the resort, she saw the possibility of her dream coming true—owning her own business. She convinced Tony and his uncle to let her buy into the project, and though she could only afford ten percent ownership, she was on her way.

Now they were two weeks away from the grand opening. It was all really happening.

No way was she letting her needy hormones muck it up.

Tony scooted out from under the desk and rose to his full height of six-foot-two. The scent of his sexy, spicy aftershave washed over her. "Let's turn it on."

She swallowed, knowing if he pushed any more of her buttons, she'd melt into a puddle at his feet. She managed to find her usual aplomb and propped her hand on her hip—a nice hip, too, in her estimation. Not that *he'd* ever noticed. "Where would that button be?"

Tony kissed the tip of her nose. "Cute, Franny."

"You're really trying to get on my nerves, aren't you?" Francesca stepped back, rubbing her nose as if she was trying to rid herself of his chaste kiss. In truth, she was tingling from her nose all the way to her toes. Ridiculous. Embarrassing. Useless.

Tony punched the power button on the computer and propped his butt—a magnificent specimen—against the desk. His velvety brown eyes danced. "Can you believe it's been almost twenty years since you slugged me in the lunchroom and demanded I come up with a cooler nickname than 'Franny'?"

"And got two days of after-school detention from Principal Duncan for my efforts."

"Hey, didn't I pull the fire alarm to get you released?"

"I'll never understand how you didn't get caught."

"I have an innocent smile," he said, then grinned.

Even at ten, he'd known how to drive women wild with his charm. Of course, she'd been unmoved. At least until the night, eight years later, when she'd accidentally walked in on him as he was getting out of the shower...

Yikes. Bad train of thought.

To distract herself, she glanced around the opulent room they'd converted to their office suite, complete with full bar and sunken living room, decorated to give an impression of class and wealth. She sighed as her gaze fell on the windowed wall to her left, beyond which lay the blossoming vineyards. She still bemoaned this valuable space Tony had commandeered on the third floor. She'd even called Joe when Tony insisted he couldn't work in an office off the lobby. But surprisingly Joe—a practical, hardworking businessman to the core—had sided with his nephew. They could use the suite to entertain potential clients and guests, he'd pronounced.

That Prince of the Universe upbringing of his would be their undoing.

The computer chimed as Windows loaded. He turned around and leaned over the desk. "Looks great, huh?"

With her gaze once again dropping to his lower half—this time catching an excellent, close-up view of that great backside of his—she nodded enthusiastically. "Oh, yeah."

"Go check your computer. I want to see if they're networked right." He tapped on the keyboard. "I'm sending you an interoffice e-mail."

"Yeah?" she said, turning her head sideways, still staring at his butt, not really interested in technology at the moment.

He glanced at her over his shoulder. "What are you doing back there?"

She yanked her gaze from his bod. Her face flushed. "I, uh— I'm going to check my e-mail." She backed out of his office and into hers.

Out of reach of temptation and the influence of his aftershave, she managed to pull herself together.

She sank into her office chair. With a simple walnut desk, chairs upholstered in dark green and her knick-knacks and diplomas hanging on the walls, her surroundings were completely different from Tony's sleek, black-marble-and-glass–appointed room. But it suited her.

The mirror on the opposite wall reflected a woman with her dark-brown hair pulled into a ponytail, an ordinary face—though she had inherited her mother's naturally tanned skin—blue eyes, and nearly-chewed-off pink lipstick. This last was no doubt a casualty of all that butt-gazing. Her mile-long to-do list lay next to her keyboard. Her in box was a good foot high.

Ah, reality. It's good to have you back.

Back from her brief foray into fantasyland, she was reminded of the life-affirming decisions she'd made recently.

She was at a point in her life where romantic flings had ceased to be a priority. She was a serious business-woman now, with major responsibilities. Tired of the commitment-wary, ambition-challenged guys she'd dated in the past, she'd decided she was holding out for Mr. Right. And Tony certainly wasn't him.

Dear Tony. Who always skated by in life, then charmed himself out of any situation he'd screwed up.

Even if he ever looked at her as anything other than a friend, she knew he wasn't The One. The One was going to walk into her life one day and she'd know, instantly, that he was the love of her life. For five generations the women in her family had fallen completely, instantly in love with their future husbands, and seeing the results of her parents' wonderful thirty-year marriage, she had no doubt love would find her the same way.

So, in conclusion, all you stubborn, Tony-dazzled hormones back off!

She pulled up her e-mail and opened the one from Tony.

Hi, *bella*. Have I told you lately I couldn't live without you?

Francesca sucked in a breath. Her hormones danced a jig.

She scrolled down further.

I'd never manage to eat a decent meal.

-T

"Did you get the message?" Tony called from the other room.

"Oh, yeah." Clamping down on her disappointment and deciding two could play at this game, she typed,

Ecstasy awaits you tonight...

Then she skipped down a few lines and added,

We're having fettuccine with scallops.

She hit the send button, rose from her chair, rolled her shoulders back, then marched from the office. The One was just around the corner, poised to save her from this impossible attraction.

He just had to be.

TONY LEANED across his desk and snagged the ringing phone. "This is Tony."

"Mr. Galini, this is Alice in reservations, I have a Mr. Pierre von Shalburg on the phone. He's making a reservation, but he insisted on speaking with you personally."

Tony searched his memory, but came up blank on anyone named von Shalburg. "Who's he?"

"I thought you'd know. He sounds important," Alice said nervously.

Shoving aside a stack of invoices he had to get through before he could join Francesca for dinner, Tony sighed. "Put him on."

How did anybody actually get any work done when people were always calling and interrupting?

This is a customer, Francesca—aka his self-appointed conscience of business responsibility—would have reminded him. *Customers come first.*

Who knew his impulsive decision to accept Uncle Joe's challenge to make something significant of his life would involve actual work and stress? He'd only become a businessman to impress the uncle he regarded so highly. He wanted people to look at him with the admiration and respect they gave Joe. Unfortunately, his resort-owner fantasy wasn't meshing with reality.

He'd pictured walking around the restaurant, smiling at patrons, offering suggestions and wine pairings. He imagined cocktail parties with plenty of lovely ladies in attendance.

But so far...zilch in the fun department. Why had he thought he could do this? He'd been perfectly happy milking his trust fund like nearly everyone else he knew. Hell, it was practically a Galini family tradition.

"This is Pierre von Shalburg," said an unfamiliar voice.

The man paused at length, giving Tony the impression that he should recognize von Whoever's name immediately. Which, of course, he didn't. He fell back on a familiar skill—bluffing. "Ah, yes. What can I do for you?" he asked as he searched the piles of paper on his desk for a pad to take notes.

Von So-and-So cleared his throat importantly. "I believe, Mr. Galini, it's what *I* can do for *you* that should be of interest to your establishment."

Really? He'd worked his ass off for nearly six months just to have his first encounter with an actual guest want to make him bang his head against the wall. He'd left jet-setting for *this?*

"Fortunately for you," the guy continued, "my schedule is free during the weekend you're planning to open." He paused. "You *are* planning to open on time, aren't you?"

Tony raised his eyebrows. "Of course." Who *was* this guy?

"I'm so thrilled for you," Mr. von Snooty said in such a deadpan voice that Tony pictured him winning the fifty-million-dollar lottery and saying, "I *suppose* this will *do.*"

"I'll arrive on Friday afternoon at precisely three o'clock. I'll require a suite with a view of the vineyards." He paused. "You do *have* rooms overlooking the vineyards, don't you?"

"Naturally." What else would they have views of?

"I want room service delivered at precisely seven o'clock in the morning..."

Sighing about the sad state of a world in which jerks like von Whatsisname existed, Tony nevertheless started scribbling notes.

"I'll inform you of my dietary requirements when I arrive and peruse the menu." He paused. "You do *have* menus, don't you?"

Tony ground his teeth. "Yes, sir, we do."

"Twelve o'clock, lunch; six o'clock, cocktails; seven o'clock, dinner. I will also require a tour of the facilities, including the winery, and, of course, a tasting."

"I'm sure we can accommodate you."

"That will be all, Mr. Galini. Expect me next Friday."

"Ye—" A dial tone sounded in his ear.

Tony slammed the phone into its cradle. "What an ass." He looked over his sparse notes and had the feeling he should have asked von Whoever-he-was more questions.

He ran a hand through his hair. What had ever possessed him to actually *make* something of his life? His friends were probably having drinks at the club about now, talking about their summer trips to Barbados. What was he doing? Sweating and stressing as he installed computers and got insulted by guys named von Something-or-Other, whom he probably could have snubbed under any other circumstances.

It was that look in Joe's eyes. That look that asked *Are you going to be a trust-fund waste like the rest of my brothers' children?* Guilt had suffused him. Guilt that apparently everyone else in his family—except two of

Joe's sons, who ran the family's Tribiletto winery in Italy—seemed conveniently to have been born without.

Was he really up to this challenge? He had zero business experience. He clearly had no patience with demanding clients. His parents called the resort "Tony's little distraction".

His friends thought he'd lost his mind and kept telling him to call a shrink whenever he had the urge to do something productive.

But sometime in the last few months, a deep desire to prove himself had stubbornly sparked to life. He wasn't selfish and spoiled like his parents. He wanted to prove everyone wrong about his ability to commit. He wanted respect. He *needed* it.

The question was—could he earn it?

First thing, though, he had to find out who von Snobby was. "Francesca!" he shouted.

A few seconds later, the intercom speaker on his desk phone beeped, then Francesca's calm voice floated out. "We spent an unmentionable amount of money on the phones, Tony, maybe we should actually use them."

And, boy, could *that* woman be bossy. "Hey," he said into the speakerphone, "I just got off the phone with this guy—do you know a Pierre von Something-or-Another?"

She drew a swift breath. "Pierre von Shalburg?"

"That's him!" He sagged in relief. "You know him. He yammered on like I should know who he is, but I didn't have a clue—"

"Oh, God. Tony, did you say you just talked to him?"

"Yeah. He yammered on—"

"What did you say?" Francesca yelled.

Scowling, Tony tapped his pen against the desk. "I said yes."

"To what exactly?"

"To him coming here for opening weekend."

A long silence ensued. Then, "You'd better meet me in the kitchen."

List in hand, he headed out of his office, down the hall and took the elevator to the kitchen. He'd been pleasant enough to the guy. Francesca acted as though he couldn't deal with a simple reservation. He hadn't exactly bubbled over with enthusiasm, though, and he doubted their guest-to-be would bend beneath his smile. Why couldn't von Shalburg have been a six-foot blonde with legs to die for?

As he approached the open doorway, he saw Francesca standing behind one of the assistant chefs—sous chefs she called them—hovering as he cooked scallops in a big frying pan. She looked tired. Her usually jaunty ponytail hung limply against her neck. Sweat glistened on her face.

Actually...He angled his head. She looked really good sweaty. Not unkempt so much as...mussed. As if she'd rolled out of a bed she hadn't wanted to leave.

He'd seen Francesca first thing in the morning many times. Throughout their teenage years, her parents had let him stay with them when his parents had gone out of town and they'd been between housekeepers— which was often, since his mother was forever accusing his father of sleeping with them, and he was always trying to make up for his behavior by taking her to Aspen or Paris or St. Croix.

That was Francesca—always around when he needed her, always willing to see him through any situation.

They had been best friends since they were ten, when Tony's parents had decided he should start attending public school on Long Island, rather than going back to boarding school in England. Years later, he'd learned this change of heart hadn't been prompted by his homesickness, but the hundred-thou-a-year his parents had saved by keeping him home.

Francesca's tongue peeked out to flick across her bottom lip, and he groaned. How would she look with her long, dark hair loose and caressing her face? The strands looked silky, but how did they feel? He couldn't recall ever gliding his hands through her hair. Why was that? Why hadn't he—

Because she's the only true friend you have.

He shook his head. What the hell was wrong with him? Erotic fantasies about Francesca? He'd definitely been working too hard.

And last night didn't count. He'd only been consoling Barbie on the breakup of her engagement.

He walked into the kitchen, then leaned against the counter. "I could use a martini."

Francesca glanced at him, her blue eyes sharp. "I'll page the bartender."

"Do we *have* a bartender?" He winced as she continued to glare. He was an owner now, not a guest. He really needed to come up with a mantra or something to help him remember that. "Hell, now I'm starting to sound like that pompous jerk."

Crossing to the industrial-sized, walk-in freezer, he headed straight for the ice-cold bottle of Grey Goose on the third shelf. He mixed his drink—and one for Francesca as well. She'd been working as hard as he had. Probably harder.

Maybe he should volunteer to take her out. She deserved a night off.

"Pompous jerk?" she asked, lifting one eyebrow. "That would be Pierre von Shalburg, I assume?"

He sampled his martini, found it nicely balanced, so he pushed the second glass across the counter to Francesca, which she picked up by the stem between her thumb and forefinger and sipped. He smiled at the elegant picture she made—even in jeans, a stained T-shirt and an apron. "That would be him," he said finally.

Eyes narrowed, she set down her martini glass with a clang. "What did you say to him?"

He cut his gaze right then left, looking for an escape. He drank again from his glass. "He pretty much did all the talking."

He thought he saw smoke seeping from Francesca's ears. "Do you have any idea who he is?" she asked.

"Well, no, not exactly."

"He's the principle critic for *A Vino* magazine."

Thank God. Finally, a name he recognized. Just last week Uncle Joe had gone on and on about the influence of the magazine, since *A Vino* was the resort industry's premier review—

Oh, hell. He leaned heavily onto the counter. "He can make us or break us."

Francesca crossed her arms over her chest. "You do have a talent for succinctness." She glared at him. "When absolutely forced beyond reason."

"I did okay. Really," he added, when she continued to stare daggers in his direction. He grasped her hands, sliding his thumbs across her skin. "I wrote down everything he said and assured him we could accommodate his every desire." He smiled. "You know how good I am at that."

To his surprise, instead of returning his smile, she scowled and pulled her hands from his grasp. "No, I don't believe I've had the pleasure."

Well, I could—

No, no, no. This is Francesca, you idiot. Your best friend.

He couldn't put any moves on her.

He wasn't a long-term guy—his personal relationship record was three months. Francesca needed more from a man. She'd told him so dozens of times. Usually after she'd broken things off with a guy who turned out to be "commitment-phobic." And if there was ever a commitment-phobic guy, it was him. Again, a Galini family tradition—with the exception of Joe and his wife. And, really, he could modestly admit to himself that he had plenty of female attention. Why limit his talents to just one? It didn't seem equitable.

Besides, he wasn't attracted to Francesca. Not at all. Not in the least.

He drained his martini. "Well, anyway, here's the

list." He pushed the scribbled note toward her. "When do we eat?"

"Any minute now." Finally giving him a quick smile, Francesca glanced over the note. "Imagine Pierre von Shalburg at *our* resort. If we can impress him, we'll have solid bookings for the next year. I'm sure the staff can handle the meal requirements. We've already been working on some grand opening specials. And Joe will be here to do the tour—"

"*I'll* do the tour."

Francesca eyed him skeptically.

"Ches, if there's anything I understand it's the vines. I've been pruning every winter and harvesting every fall since I was fourteen."

She held up her hand. "I know, I know. Sorry."

"Dinner, Ms. D'Arcy," the sous chef announced, setting two plates on the counter in front of him and Francesca.

"Thank you, Kerry," she said.

The scent of sautéed scallops wafted past him, and Tony put all thoughts of the cranky Pierre von Shalburg out of his mind. He selected a '96 chardonnay from the fridge and poured the straw-colored liquid into two glasses. He paused with the bottle hovering over a third glass. "Kerry?"

"No, thank you, sir," the sous chef said, wiping sweat from his brow with a towel. "I still have prep work for tomorrow."

Tony set aside the bottle, then picked up his glass. He touched the crystal to Francesca's. "To success."

They had been eating like this, standing at the counter in the warm, busy kitchen in the basement, nearly every night for a month. Tony found himself checking his watch in the afternoon in anticipation of dinner with her. Must be a latent longing for all those impersonal meals he'd endured growing up with nobody but the housekeeper for company.

As they enjoyed the delicious meal, they discussed plans for the critic's visit.

With the number of resorts in the area growing, they'd had to find ways to distinguish themselves from the competition. Since the wine production had always been their focus, it seemed logical to focus on food, wine and music, rather than spa services.

Would von Shalburg participate in their planned cooking classes?

Tony doubted it.

Would he relax in the jazz-themed bar at night?

Maybe. But certainly alone.

Would he like the wine-pairing sessions?

Only if he could tell everybody what he thought and have them bow and definitively agree with every word he said.

Finally, frustrated, Francesca shoved her plate aside. "Well, what do *you* think he would like?"

"How about a day at the spa? We could foist him off on Chateau Fontaine down the road."

Francesca sighed. "No, do you plan to shuffle off *every* troublesome guest?"

"Hmm…Yes?"

"No." She leaned toward him. "We're trying to attract all the guests we can handle. Bookings equal revenue, remember? As much as you obviously don't want to admit it, we *need* Pierre von Shalburg. He could bring us industry buzz and accreditation."

"He could bring us a giant pain in the—"

"We agreed we were going to give this our best shot."

Tony hung his head. He'd agreed all right—to the coup sponsored by Francesca and Uncle Joe.

No, that wasn't true—or fair. Fact was, in addition to being one of the few Galinis in his generation capable of guilt, he'd also been a complete sucker for the hope and resolve that had shone in Francesca's eyes that fateful day six months ago.

She'd always had so much faith in him—faith that he could get through his English final in high school, faith that he could graduate college, faith that he could resist Tiffani Lambeau's determined advances even though she claimed her new husband ignored her, and, more recently, faith that he would be the best, most charming resort host on Long Island.

"Has it really been all that bad?" she asked softly.

Startled, he lifted his head. "No, of course not." And it hadn't. Watching the resort go from mere drawings on a page to three-dimensional reality, having people listen to his opinion on something besides which was the hip nightclub this month had been great. The responsibility gave him a sense of belonging and acceptance he hadn't anticipated.

He just kept waiting for the whole thing to fall apart. No one—save Joe and Francesca—expected him to succeed. Not his acquaintances, his parents or his friends. He, in fact, knew they all had a pool going on the precise moment his dismal failure as a business-man would occur.

At least he'd cost that joker Sonny Compton—who'd started the pool—two hundred bucks already.

Francesca slid her hand over his. "You *can* do this."

He stared into her sparkling, earnest blue eyes and almost believed her.

She was the only one who knew of his need to prove he wasn't like his parents, that he could be a success in business—or anything else. He also suspected she knew he was terrified of everything he had to do in order to provide that proof....

He gripped her hand tightly. "I can't thank you enough—"

"Don't, Tony. I didn't do anything, and I should be thanking you. I could never have jumped into the business at this level without you and your connections."

"The only reason Joe offered to let me into the project was because he knew I'd turn to you for help."

She shook her head, and tendrils of long, dark hair brushed her cheeks. "That's not true."

He thought it was, but he wasn't particularly interested in examining Joe's motives at the moment. He'd rather look into Francesca's eyes. He'd rather stroke his thumb across her palm, feel the warmth of her skin, feel her pulse race in time with his. He'd rather brush her hair away from her cheek.

As if in a dream he did all these things, when he should have kept his hands to himself and his thoughts under control.

As his hand cupped her face, her breath came in short gasps. Her spicy, fruity scent enveloped him. He licked his lips, imaging the taste of her—wine and butter and something that would be hers and hers alone.

He glided his other hand to her waist. He leaned forward.

"What the hell are you doing?"

2

STUNNED, Francesca stared at Tony, at the glazed, desire-filled look in his eyes. She felt as if the world had suddenly starting spinning in a different direction.

He jerked his head and his hands back. "I—I've got to run." He drained his wineglass, then stepped away from the counter.

She acutely felt the loss of his warmth, but since she'd so rudely drawn attention to his touch in the first place, she didn't see how she could ask him to come back. "Run?"

"Out." He grabbed her plate and his, then rinsed them both in the sink before putting them in the dishwasher. "To uh—I'm going up to...to the chateau."

"Fontaine?" she asked, still confused about his odd behavior.

"Yeah. Meeting some friends." He smiled, holding out his hands. "You know me, unending social life."

Yeah, she did, and she was getting damn sick of it. She slogged away late into the night, while he took off for fun at least five nights a week. "We have work to do."

"It'll keep till morning."

"What about the invoices?"

"Almost done. I'll catch up tomorrow."

"No, Tony—"

"I'll see you in the morning. Coffee in the lobby?"

Since they'd been doing that for weeks, she nodded.

He leaned forward as if he was going to brush her cheek with his lips as usual, but she felt only a puff of breath against her skin. Giving her an odd look, he jumped back.

And, before she could even fully register the fact that he was leaving, he'd scooted across the room.

She watched him—specifically his great butt—as he disappeared around the corner.

Prince Galini has left the building.

She sighed. How could she be annoyed with him and still desire him? The transition to working every day had been hard for him, she knew, but his lack of commitment was getting old.

What did you expect, girl? That twenty-eight years of hedonism and indulgence were going to disappear overnight?

It was probably better he was gone. With him also went his disturbing effect on her.

She knew one thing for sure—The One had better hurry his late ass into her life soon, or she was going to burn up from the inside out.

With effort, she focused her brain on a safer topic. Pierre von Shalburg would do nicely. As much as Tony complained—a trait inherited from his spoiled parents, which Tony had, she was thankful, only a touch of— she was ready to jump up and down with the coup of having the influential critic attend their opening weekend. She wasn't worried about his eccentricities or demands. Par for the course in the hotel business. The challenge of impressing the critic and getting Bella

Luna on his Top Picks far outweighed the fear of a possible poor review.

Spurred into action by the opportunity, she cast a quick good-night over her shoulder to Kerry and headed upstairs to her office. She went online and searched for articles and reviews written by von Shalburg, cross-referencing them for commonly mentioned ingredients, favored presentation of dishes and service comments. She learned he liked all kinds of seafood—convenient, since Francesca had found a fabulous fish supplier. Shalburg was also a respected sommelier and could spot a weak wine with one sniff. He favored delicate and savory as opposed to overly spicy food, and he liked his service unobtrusive and as silent as possible—no surprise, given Tony's "pompous jerk" assessment.

She rubbed her hands together. Now, what recipe could she come up with to wow him?

The phone rang before she'd managed to consider even one entrée.

When she answered, a familiar voice asked, "How's my angel?"

"Hi, Dad," Francesca returned, smiling as she leaned back in her chair. "How's Palm Springs?"

Her father had owned a bakery while she was growing up, but he'd sold the business a few years ago, and he and her mother had spent much of that time traveling. Francesca was glad to see them relax and enjoy retirement. While they'd never lacked for anything during her childhood, they'd never had anything close to the financial freedom of Tony's family or many of the other families whose children had attended her school.

They'd put every spare penny into buying a house in a mostly posh area so she could get a great education, and the longer she spent in the "real world," the more she appreciated their sacrifice.

"Great. Weather's primo. I beat your mother today at golf."

"She let you, you know."

He sighed. "I know, but she loves me enough to let me win occasionally."

"Just remember, Dad, she can't even make a decent PB and J."

"Why would anybody put jelly on first and try to spread peanut butter on top of that?"

Francesca laughed at the memory. "Got me."

She caught her father up on the busy week and assured him she couldn't wait for their visit on the second weekend after the resort opened. With the critic's visit imminent, Francesca was glad she hadn't insisted on having her parents for the grand opening and had instead taken her dad's advice that she didn't need the added pressure of family underfoot.

"Dad, thanks for giving me a great business sense," she said after the update.

"And how is Tony?"

"I wasn't comparing myself to Tony."

"Oh, yes, you were."

"No, I—"

"Tony has his own strengths, angel. He has a great sense of what people need."

What they need? Oh, God, if he sensed what she really needed from him—to satisfy a gnawing itch of desire that had taken up residence in her body and refused to leave—she'd die of embarrassment.

"...that charm of his is legendary," her father continued. "*He* could charm your mother into letting him win *every* golf match."

It didn't help her case against Tony that her father had always favored him. He'd always hoped she'd turn her interest to Tony and "bring him around." Like a wary stallion, she assumed.

"I'm sure he could, Dad," she said.

"I know you're busy. I'll let you go."

She pushed aside her worry about Tony, the business and everything else. She missed her dad. Missed his guidance and clear head. "I'm never too busy for you."

They talked a bit longer, and as she finished the phone call, she was smiling, but the smile faded as her father's words came back to her—*his charm is legendary.* She needed to remember that whenever she got weak. Whenever she was tempted to fantasize about Tony's butt. Or his smile. Or the charming way he always managed to be the center of attention.

Professionally, she wanted a successful resort. Personally, she *didn't* want an affair. She *wanted* a life partner, a love for a lifetime. And Tony, Mr. New-Blonde-Every-Saturday-Night, didn't come close to qualifying.

Closing her eyes against her troubles, she leaned her head back against her office chair. And—for some reason—a vision of Tony's hands drifted through her mind.

She couldn't explain it, to herself or anyone else, but his hands turned her on. She was fascinated with them.

Being a man of six feet tall, his hands were large, his fingers long. A bit of dark hair touched his knuckles. His sporty silver watch was perpetually wrapped around his wrist, highlighting his tanned skin.

Nothing unusual really.

Yet, she couldn't stop thinking about the strength—and the pleasure—those hands could surely induce. Tony was never at a loss for female companionship. What ecstasy could those practiced hands bring? Would his touch be sure and relentless? Or soft and tentative? Or...*both?*

She forced her eyes open. Work, that's what she needed. More and more work. These wild feelings for Tony would pass. They'd never been this intense before, had they? She'd always been able to talk herself out of an attraction to him. And she would again.

She hoped.

She had to.

"Thanks, Paul. I appreciate the lift home."

Paul saluted and bounced the keys to Tony's Mercedes in his palm. "No problem, Mr. Galini. I'm glad to drive your baby anytime."

Tony cast a longing look at his car idling in the driveway. He'd been at Chateau Fontaine, drinking and socializing. In truth, he'd had little to drink, but he'd let time get away from him—as usual—and had stayed later than he planned. With the long work hours, he was plain exhausted, and he hadn't wanted to drive himself back to Bella Luna, even over the mere mile separating the two properties.

He was dead on his feet, and his last, semi-conscious concern was for his car.

"Take care of her, Paul. I'll call you and arrange a time to retrieve her tomorrow." He slid a folded fifty-dollar bill into the valet's palm. "Remind me to tell your boss about your invaluable service."

"You bet, Mr. G." Paul saluted again, walking backwards towards the car. "That redhead wanted you, man. I'm tellin' ya. I can get her room number if you want it."

Tony yawned. This working for a living was hell on his social life. "Um-hmm. Maybe tomorrow."

Paul and the Mercedes slid out of the horseshoe-shaped drive as Tony unlocked the front door and entered the lobby. Normally, he paused to gaze into the starlit sky, of which the glass dome over the lobby afforded him an unrestricted view, but tonight he shuffled his feet across the cream-tiled floor and headed straight for the elevator.

He'd share coffee with Francesca in the morning and enjoy the sunlight instead.

Francesca.

He leaned his forehead against the elevator wall, reliving the surprised, almost horrified look on her face when he'd nearly kissed her in the kitchen earlier.

What in the world was wrong with him?

Thankfully, the elevator doors opened, saving him from reliving that exciting, wonderful, awful moment. Again.

Eyes half closed, he stumbled down the third-floor hall, only to curse softly when he reached into his pocket to find it keyless.

He leaned back against his door. Maybe he could just sleep in the hallway. He gazed blearily down at the Cabernet-colored carpet beneath his tasseled loafers. He really needed his cushiony-soft down-feathered pillow, but he didn't want to wake anybody up, least of all Francesca, though she was in the room right next door. The sight of her mussed and sleepy-eyed, clad in whatever big, baggy T-shirt she wore to bed would overload his already weak system.

But then some part of his still-functioning brain—and where was *that* part earlier when he'd been gazing at his best friend as though she was a steak and he a vegetarian who'd fallen off the wagon?—reminded him about the key code. They'd had electronic, numeric key pads installed at each door, so guests could set their own codes and enter their rooms without keys.

His idea. And, if he must say, a brilliant one.

He opened one eye long enough to input his code—the day he and Francesca had met in the fourth grade—then opened the door with a sigh of relief.

In the dark, he kicked off his shoes, then stripped off his clothes. Naked, he crawled into bed. He was asleep before his head sank fully into his plush feather pillow.

FRANCESCA MOANED in the middle of an erotic dream.

Starring Tony.

Part of her thought this was a really bad idea, but that part was quickly overridden by the warm, confident, male hand gliding up her waist to cup her satin-clad breast.

She arched her back, pressing her body more firmly

against his, her fingers stroking his trim, muscled sides, smiling at the weight of his body on hers, at the hard ridge of male flesh pressed against her middle.

As she slid her hands lower, she found bare skin. Oh, God, he was naked. How many nights had she lain awake imagining Tony naked? That one glimpse at eighteen hadn't been nearly enough. And since then he'd…filled out quite a bit. He was a couple of inches taller, his shoulders were broader. Where else, exactly, had he grown?

A wicked giggle escaped her mouth at the thought.

He trailed his lips over her throat, then sank his teeth lightly into her earlobe. "Ah, *bella*, I love to hear you laugh."

She trailed her fingers across his bare butt.

He sucked in a quick breath. "I like that even better." He flicked his thumb over her burgeoning nipple, then impatiently pushed up her camisole.

Heat flooded her body, the very blood in her veins. She slid her hand up his back, threading her fingers through the wavy hair at the base of his neck, urging him on. A hunger she didn't think could ever be satisfied had begun to grow deep within. She wanted his touch, craved his attention. She wanted all that charm and energy and expertise focused on her. And her alone.

She recalled her thoughts earlier about his hands; those hands were currently stroking her flesh, sending her nerve endings on a crazy roller-coaster ride….

His mouth captured hers, his tongue slid past her lips, confidence and seduction inherent in every move. He was warm and tasted like…like…

Like cigar smoke?

Not in this fantasy, buster.

The odd smell brought her fully awake. Tony was indeed in her bed. And naked. And currently trailing his fabulous mouth across her chest.

Oh, hell.

HEART POUNDING, Francesca shoved Tony's shoulder. "Tony!"

He didn't seem to hear her. His mouth reached her nipple. His tongue flicked across the distended peak.

Francesca gasped. Oh, heavens, he was even better at this than she'd imagined. A steady, insistent throbbing pounded between her legs. Longing filled her belly. She'd wanted him for so long...

No. Not like this. Not when he wouldn't even remember anything. When he probably didn't even know who she was.

Knowing she had to wake him up, she shoved his shoulder again. His tongue flicked again.

Moaning, she wrapped her legs around his waist—and, oh wow, his erection pressed harder against her—then flipped him over onto his back. She reached over to the bedside table and turned on the light for good measure.

He blinked in the sudden pool of brightness. "Ches?"

Her heart was racing, and her body throbbed. Still, she managed to raise her hand. "Present."

He propped himself up on his elbows. "What's—" He stopped, his gaze sliding from her face to her body.

"Holy—" His gaze jerked back to hers. Lust shone from his chocolate-colored eyes.

Vowing she wouldn't revel in his admiration, Francesca yanked the strap of her camisole back onto her shoulder, covering her naked breast. His erection pulsed beneath her, reminding her that she still straddled him—and that she excited him. She closed her eyes and forced herself to slide off his aroused, luscious body and stand next to the bed.

Mmm. Good move, sister.

Still not fully awake, Tony clearly hadn't realized she wasn't the only one not dressed decently. He, in fact, wasn't dressed at all, and she couldn't resist a long, leisurely stare down his body. He had wide shoulders, trim arms and a muscled chest and stomach, all of which she'd seen at the country-club pool many times over the last several years, and which were evidence of his devotion to exercise and lifting weights.

But then her curious gaze hit on his...other parts. Parts she hadn't seen in a long, great while. Parts that wanted her.

Oh, yeah, he'd grown all right. And was continuing to gr—

"Ches?"

She jerked her gaze back to his. He'd banked the lust, and now she saw mostly confusion. What was she doing ogling him?

"I, uh—" She went for indignation. "What are you doing in my room?"

He snatched the comforter over his body. "Your

room? This is my—'' He stopped as he looked around. ''This is your room.''

Thanking heaven she'd managed to compose herself, she crossed her arms over her chest. ''And you're here because...?''

He leapt off the bed, wrapping the bed covers around his waist. ''I thought— What are you wearing?''

She raised her eyebrows. ''My pajamas.'' She flicked her gaze toward the digital clock. ''It's 2:00 a.m. What else should I be wearing?''

''A T-shirt,'' he muttered, dragging his hand through his already mussed hair.

''Why—'' She stopped and glanced down at herself. Okay, so maybe the hot-pink satin was a bit much. A T-shirt probably suited practical, business-savvy Francesca D'Arcy better, but, hey, a girl couldn't be practical *all* the time.

Still, she grabbed her robe from the hook over the bathroom door. It matched the pajamas, so it didn't cover much, but she felt slightly more practical wearing it.

With the bulky comforter around him, Tony waddled across the room, then through the doorway and into the living area of the suite. ''I'll just, uh, get my pants.''

Francesca watched him go, the gold-colored comforter a stark contrast to his tanned shoulders and back. *Whoa, baby.*

Knees weak, she sank onto the edge of the bed. The bed where she and Tony had just rounded second base, cruising their way rapidly to third.

She leapt to her feet. Bed bad. Pacing good.

She'd barely begun her fourth pass across the room, trying to figure out what to say to her best friend and how to say it, when his voice startled her from her thoughts.

"I didn't realize dreams *literally* came true."

Her heart thudded. "What?"

"One minute I'm dreaming about us, and the next...I'm not dreaming, but living."

She turned toward him as he leaned one shoulder against the doorframe. He'd put on his black pants and white shirt, though he'd left the shirt unbuttoned. The trim muscles on his chest peeked tantalizingly through the opening. "Me, too," she said quietly.

He cocked his head. "Weird, huh?"

She sighed—with relief or disappointment, she wasn't sure. "Oh, yeah."

"How do you feel about what just...what just almost happened?"

She groaned. How was a woman supposed to resist a man concerned about how she *felt?* "I'm not sure," she said. "How about you?"

"I look at you, and I see my good buddy Ches, but—" his gaze flicked toward the bed "—then I remember...."

"Yeah." At least he wouldn't have to sleep in that bed every night.

They stared at each other from across the room. Most people might assume Tony was relaxed, as he was propped against the doorway and smiling. But Francesca knew him better than probably anybody—his moods, his gestures, his dreams, even his lies.

Tony was troubled.

His smile was forced. His posture stiff. His erection unabated.

He straightened suddenly. "Well, this is damned awkward."

Just what she'd feared. Every time she'd thought about admitting she desired him as more than a friend, this is what she pictured—laughing, teasing, charming Tony replaced by a pensive, awkward stranger.

"Yeah" was all she said.

"Maybe it will be different in the morning."

"Maybe." Though she didn't see how. She knew his touch now. *Imagining* the sparks they'd create was a great deal different than actually experiencing them. She knew she'd never be able to look at him the same way, and she doubted he would either.

The idea filled her with sadness. They'd weathered many crises in the past. They had to find a way past this, too.

"I think I'll go back to bed," he said. "In my own room this time."

She nodded. "That's probably best."

He walked toward the door, and she followed him, wondering what she could say to change things, to go back, to make him comfortable with her again, but she felt as though she was hanging on an emotional precipice, and she was fresh out of rational, practical ideas.

As he pulled open the door, he looked back at her. "You know what this means, don't you?"

Oh, God. They couldn't be friends anymore? They couldn't be business partners?

"We chose the same access number—the day we met." He paused. "Weird, huh?"

Knowing she couldn't take much more upheaval, she let go of the breath she'd been holding. "Definitely."

He yanked her to him, laying a quick, hard kiss on her forehead. And, somehow, she felt passion, regret and strength all in that one gesture. "Night, Ches."

"Night." She closed the door, then banged her head lightly against the hard metal surface.

3

TRAY OF COFFEE and fresh croissants in hand, Tony paused in the lobby solarium.

Nope. Still couldn't see her without picturing her in that pink silky thing she slept in. He'd thought for sure he'd wrestled his attraction into submission early this morning.

He couldn't sleep, so he'd decided to talk some sense into himself.

Risking nineteen years of friendship just to assuage his lust was a *bad* idea. Screwing up his business partnership—the one chance he had to prove he could succeed at something besides clubbing—was an even worse idea. He liked women. He didn't obsess about them. He simply enjoyed them—in and out of bed. He wasn't an animal, after all.

He was a man.

A man who wanted a woman beyond reason.

A woman he shouldn't, *couldn't* have.

"Is this what we're reduced to?" she asked suddenly, turning to stare at him over her shoulder. "Avoiding each other? At a loss for words?"

Tony forced a smile and continued the last several feet to the wicker chair where Francesca sat. "I'm not avoiding you," he said firmly, setting the tray on the table in front of her.

"You were just standing there trying to figure out how to tell me we're out of Irish breakfast tea?"

He sat, then poured her a cup, using the delicate china he'd brought her from London two years ago. "I was wondering how to approach you. You look like you're wearing armour this morning."

She took the cup and saucer, adding milk and sweetener, then she glanced down at herself. "I don't know what you're talking about."

"You're wearing a turtleneck, Ches."

She sipped her tea, not meeting his gaze. "It's cold."

"In Alaska." He leaned back in his chair. "Here, on Long Island, in late May, it's due to be a balmy seventy-five by noon."

"So at noon, I'll change."

Even in a white turtleneck, jeans and a navy blazer, she was lovely. Fresh and sexy. And—

Off-limits.

The clothes and her stiff posture made it plain what her attitude about last night was—*I don't want to talk about it.*

Fine by him. He wanted to forget the whole thing, too.

"How does the menu for von Nose-in-the-Air look?" he asked.

She narrowed her eyes. "It's von Shalburg, and you'd better start practicing it, since you're going to be following him around saying, 'Yes, Mr. von Shalburg.' 'Whatever you say, Mr. von Shalburg.'"

"Surely, I don't have to—"

"Oh, yes. You do."

Tony sighed. When did he get to compliment and

dance with the ladies? When did he get to have cocktail parties in the owners' suite? When did he get to sip wine on the veranda?''

''Work first; fun later,'' she said, as if she'd read his thoughts.

''Much later,'' he grumbled.

''Now, what do you think of the menu?'' She pushed a sheet of paper across the table. ''I need some help with wine pairings.''

He studied the suggestions. At least wine he understood. ''I'll okay it with the sommelier, but personally, I think the '96 chardonnay was excellent with the fettuccine and scallops last night, so that's a definite yes. Adding shrimp, mussels and basil is a nice touch.''

''I'm thinking we'll use that dish for the cooking classes, too.''

''Mmm. Good idea. The grilled teriyaki salmon and asparagus could also take a chardonnay. Maybe a younger one—the '99, I think.

''Of course, the Italian trio of spaghetti, baked ziti and lasagna has to go with the Chianti—really any year. We haven't made an unremarkable one yet.''

Finished, he glanced at Francesca and found her smiling at him.

''I couldn't do this without you, you know.''

''Without my money, you mean.''

She blinked in surprise. Tony longed to call his bitter words back. He didn't resent his family money. He knew he was immensely blessed, and it was selfish and childish to think otherwise. He just wished he'd made *some* kind of contribution to his by-birth windfall.

Francesca slid her hand over his. ''Without *you*.''

He gripped her hand. "You know I don't mean to complain. I'm just— Commitment isn't my strong suit."

Her blue eyes went soft, and maybe a bit regretful, as if she realized they weren't just talking about the resort anymore. "I know."

He'd vowed just minutes ago to forget all about her and that pink silky thing, and he would, just as soon as he made sure they were on the same page in this. "Last night was an honest mistake, right? We've both been working a lot, keeping late nights and stuff."

She looked relieved. "Exactly."

"Your faith in me and your friendship mean everything. I'm not going to do anything to risk that."

"Me either."

Whew. He should have known he didn't have to worry about practical Francesca getting all caught up in the emotion of last night—as he had.

But not anymore. He reminded himself if he hadn't bailed out on working last night, everything would have turned out very differently. "I'm determined to help this resort succeed. We're going to make this work."

"Of course we are." She let go of his hand, then directed her attention to the legal pad in her lap. "You have to last at least through the summer, so I can win the pool from Sonny Compton."

"Ha, ha."

She stood, tucking her pad under her arm. "Let's take a walk outside. The concrete people are pouring the swimming pool deck this morning, and I want to see how it's going."

He rose as well. "That's my kind of pool. I'll even volunteer to be the first one to take a dip."

She linked arms with him, and her old, easy smile returned. "Let's wait a couple of days until the deck dries, okay?"

"Since I don't want to be a permanent fixture at the pool, I think I'll take that advice."

They strolled across the lobby, through the French doors to the veranda. In the last week, the landscaping company had added huge terra-cotta urns filled with ferns, ivy and bright geraniums. The scent of rosebushes and fruit trees filled the air. Their perfume washed over him, reminding him of the delicate fruity fragrance that always clung to Francesca.

Oh, no, you don't. If you have to think of a woman, think of Barbie, her broken engagement, her big blue eyes, the sway of her jeans-clad backside as she wandered over to one of the roses and inhaled the—

No, no. *Francesca* had blue eyes; Barbie had—

Actually he had no idea what color Barbie's eyes were. He'd find out. Yes. Absolutely.

And Francesca's curvy backside was off-limits. Strictly.

He forced his gaze from Francesca and focused on the truck churning out mushy cement near the still-empty pool. Men in work boots and shovels spread the mixture of cement and smooth stones in between wooden rails that laid out the path of the deck, then the sidewalk that would wind through the flower and herb garden.

Off to the side stood a familiar figure wearing worn overalls, his silver hair glinting in the sun. Uncle Joe.

Pride filled Tony at the realization that he was going to earn his uncle's respect and help fulfill his long-held dream to reach even more people with the Galini family hospitality. Tony knew he'd inherited his ease with people and his love of socializing from Joe. He respected his uncle as he did no one else and yearned for Joe's admiration in return.

During the resort's construction, Joe had arranged to incorporate the new venture into the advertising campaign he'd recently launched with Matt and Jillian Davidson to promote the Galini-label wines along with their century-old Tribiletto label worldwide. Throughout it all, Joe had never stopped running the winery and gift shop in the old farmhouse on the vineyards' west side.

His energy was boundless, a quality Tony knew he should take note of and remember the next time he had the urge to complain about his own schedule.

"Oh, there's Joe," Francesca said, waving. "Hey, Joe!"

Joe waved back, then slogged through the mud toward them. "*Ciao*," he said, kissing Francesca on the cheek. He pulled Tony to his chest for a brief hug. "I got your message, *bella*. Pierre von Shalburg, eh? Quite a triumph."

Smiling, Francesca shook her head. "I can't imagine who could have managed to arrange such a thing."

Joe winked. "Somebody powerful, I'll bet."

"Handsome, too," Tony added.

Joe laughed. "Don't forget charming."

"And with an irresistibly sexy nephew."

Francesca rolled her eyes. "Good grief."

"So, *bella*, what do you have planned to knock off Mr. von Shalburg's shoes?"

"That's socks, sir," Tony said. Joe was forever getting American expressions mixed up.

"Socks?" he asked with a confused frown.

"You step into someone's shoes, and knock someone's socks off."

Joe waved his hand. "*Sì.* So, where's the menu?"

Francesca handed a paper to him, and he took a few moments to examine the dishes. "Excellent, though you may want to add an exotic or expensive ingredient or two—maybe caviar or truffles with the salad course. That Shalburg fellow is something of a snoot-head."

Francesca frowned. Tony laughed.

"I got that one wrong, too, eh? Hmm, I meant aristocratic, high and mighty—"

Tony stopped laughing long enough to say, "No, you got it right, Uncle Joe. Snooty is, in fact, *exactly* the right description for good ole von Shalburg."

Francesca planted her hands on her hips. "You're not helping, Joe."

"What did I say?"

Tony laid his arm across his uncle's shoulders. "She's just a little uptight about von Snoothead's visit."

"I didn't get much sleep last night either," she added before thinking, then glanced at Tony. Her face flushed to the roots of her hair.

Tony couldn't help remembering the image of her stretched out on the bed, one silky, perfect breast exposed, her curvy body and olive-toned skin enticingly set off by her pink satin camisole. Desire slammed into him with the force of a stormy wind off Long Island

Sound. He swallowed. "Yeah. There's a lot of that going around."

"Let's go over by the pool and see how the pouring is coming along." Not looking at Tony, she stepped out of her heeled sandals and into a pair of rubber boots that looked as if they'd just fallen from the pages of the L.L. Bean catalog.

Tony glanced down at his Italian leather loafers and winced.

"Where are your work boots?" Joe asked.

"What would I want a pair of work boots for?" He pointed at Francesca's feet. "Especially ones as ugly as that."

Francesca and Joe exchanged an exasperated look.

Tony just shrugged, then rolled up his black pants. He balanced himself on the wooden frame for the sidewalk and used it like a tightrope to walk to the pool.

He, Joe and Francesca introduced themselves to the site foreman, but as the others discussed the mix ratio of concrete to stone, Tony gazed at the still-empty pool. Francesca would look great stretched out by the pool, wearing nothing but a bikini, sunglasses and a smile. What color would her bikini be? He recalled a red one from last summer when he and a bunch of their friends had rented a house on Martha's Vineyard.

Or maybe pink, like the now-infamous nightie.

She'd smile and turn toward him, sliding her hand up his bare thigh.

No, she'd probably just glare at him. *No that's what she's doing now, you idiot.*

He rubbed his hands together, as if he'd be glad to

volunteer to spread the concrete himself—if only he was properly dressed. "Well, it looks great to me."

Francesca promptly turned back to the concrete conversation, and he fought against the provocative images of her and her bikini. He stared—hard—at her white turtleneck.

Nope. That didn't help. He knew what was under there. He'd touched and sampled what was under there. If only he could get under there again...

"Ms. D'Arcy!" someone called from a distance.

They all turned toward the veranda.

The housekeeping manager, Mabel, waved, but she wasn't smiling. "It's Chef Carlos."

Now that man would put just about anybody off their pleasant thoughts.

FRANCESCA had barely cleared the kitchen door when the resort's prized, can't-run-the-place-without-him chef jabbed his knife into the chopping block.

"I will not work with that, that imbecile, that klutz, that...food masochist!"

Chef Carlos was half Cuban and half Puerto Rican, so to describe him as passionate was an extreme understatement. He was also highly respected, a perfectionist, well-traveled, sophisticated, and a Ricky Martin lookalike.

Since Francesca had known him only by reputation before interviewing him last month, his appearance had been something of a shock, but that was nothing compared to actually dealing with him and his...*problem* on a daily basis. In public, "fans" followed him around, they screamed, they tore at his clothes. Explaining he was not the internationally known entertainer was useless.

Even in the privacy of the resort, the problems continued. Francesca had gone through endless interviews with housekeeping managers before she'd found practical, sixty-something Mabel, who didn't want to jump him, just mother him. And Carlos himself didn't help much. Personality-wise he had little in common with the butt-shaking performer—he was a grouch, and his perfectionist nature had everyone jumpy and irritable.

"My art requires at least a *minute* bit of assisted skill. As much as I'm able to juggle, I cannot withstand the pressure *entirely* alone."

"Of course, Chef," she said, though she didn't agree with his assessment of Kerry, whom she thought was a talented, *even-tempered* sous chef.

Chef Carlos heaved a deep sigh. "What do I expect with such a child?"

"Kerry is twenty-three, Chef. He's an adult." Carlos hadn't had such a prestigious job at that age. Maybe there was a bit of jealousy here as well.

"I want him out."

But she *couldn't* get rid of Kerry. He had the secret stash of Hawaiian gourmet chocolate to make her favorite midnight snack—chocolate-covered marshmallows. He refused to reveal his source, and she couldn't make it through the night without those marshmallows. "No," she said simply.

"*No?* Did you say no? No one tells the great—"

"Oh, come on, Chef." Francesca tapped her foot. "What did he do—specifically, without histrionics?"

Francesca figured very few people ever argued with

the talented chef, but if she didn't let him know early on that she wouldn't be bullied, she'd be dealing with scenes like this every week, hell, maybe every day. With von Shalburg's visit as well as their opening round of guests just a few days away, she had to establish leadership and strength now or she wouldn't ever be able to. Still, her heart pounded with the idea that Chef Carlos might pack up his knives and go home.

"He...he cut the carrots for the pasta primavera a quarter-inch too short."

"He—" Francesca leaned against the counter for support. Life had really been okay at the Hilton. She'd had a perfectly nice job, a perfectly nice paycheck... distance from an unreasonable attraction to her best friend.

This is your dream, angel. Make it work.

She could all but hear her father whisper encouragement in her ear.

"Where is he?" she asked after a bracing roll of her shoulders.

"Here, Ms. D'Arcy," a low voice answered from the back door. Kerry held a cardboard produce box in front of his body like a shield. "I didn't mean to eavesdrop. It just sort of happened."

Francesca hurt for him. He was so quiet and tenderhearted. The food business was tough, and she worried about him being able to survive in a world where Pierre von Shalburgs and Chef Carloses flourished.

"Let's see if we can't work this out," she said.

Encouraged, Kerry took a few, halting steps forward. "Yes, ma'am."

"Food is as much about presentation as it is taste.

Chef Carlos is well known for his perfectionism. If you have to pull out a ruler to make the cuts exact, then do it."

Kerry nodded and made a small mewing sound. Carlos lifted his chin.

"And, Chef Carlos, remember, these last few days before opening are for *practice*. There's no need to berate Kerry for a small mistake. Nurture him. He'll help you look like the genius you are."

Carlos inclined his head. Kerry mewed again.

Crisis number one of the day averted. Hallelujah. She glanced at her watch. Nearly ten o'clock. How long before the next bump in the road appeared? Oh, probably about as long as it took for Tony to appear and—

"What *is* that mewing sound?"

Kerry's face flushed. "I, uh...found them in the herb garden." He extended the box he held.

With her stomach churning, Francesca approached him. Even Chef Carlos wandered over to see the box's contents.

A mother calico cat and three tiny kittens lay inside.

The blood drained from Francesca's face. *Cats?* In a commercial kitchen? Cats equaled rats according to the health department, not to mention, Chef Carlos would probably blow another gasket—

"How adorable!" Carlos exclaimed.

Francesca stared at him in shock just as the lights went out.

As THE SUN disappeared over the horizon outside, Francesca used a flashlight to make her way upstairs to Tony's office. She collapsed into the chair in front of his desk. "We should have power tomorrow. Thank God for the back-up generators. At least we don't have to worry about the food spoiling."

With the exterior floodlights reflecting off the windows and a pair of candles sitting on either end of Tony's desk, she had just enough light to see his smile flash. "I knew you'd get to the bottom of everything."

"Oh, I don't know if I got to the bottom of anything. The power company claims there was a snafu in setting up our account, but when I pointed out we've had power for a month now, the representative just said 'oh.'" Francesca shook her head, which had been throbbing since about 10:00 a.m. "I didn't see the point in arguing. I asked her if she showed a balance on our account, she said no, so I told her it sure would be nice to actually get what we'd paid for, and she promised it would be on again by eight tomorrow."

"A.m. or p.m.?"

"Who knows?" She sighed, frustrated. "Oh, and watch for saucers of milk on the kitchen floor."

"Saucers of milk?"

"We have a family of cats as our first guests. Though I hope not long enough for the health inspector to notice."

Tony clasped his hands and leaned forward. She wanted to rest her head on his chest and hold on to him more than she wanted to do just about anything.

Except maybe rip his clothes from his body.

"The sidewalk and pool deck look nice," he said.

"Zippy."

"Uncle Joe loved your menu ideas."

"Double zippy."

Tony rose, walked around the desk, then stood behind her. He slid his hands over her shoulders, squeezing the muscles. "You're incredible, you know."

Perilously close to tears, Francesca closed her eyes. "Maybe I'm not cut out for this."

Tony's hands clenched. "You were *born* for this."

"It's just so different when it's yours. When I left the Hilton at night, I could set aside the problems, I could even laugh away the craziness. Now, I'm just so damn edgy and nervous—"

"Stop," he said next to her ear. He grabbed the chair by the arms and spun her to face him, leaning over her until she could feel his breath on her face as he spoke. "This is a blip in the road, a low in your tide. And just think how awful it's going to be once von Snooty gets here."

Her gaze flicked to his. Laughter gurgled up from her diaphragm. She leaned forward, resting her forehead on his chest as she let the giggles escape. She was just tired. Last night, no sleep as she tortured herself with thoughts of her and Tony's bodies sliding together. Today, one crisis after another. And here she was, in the dark, alone with him as candles flickered across their faces. Touching him, inhaling him.

She stopped laughing when he stroked his hand down the back of her head. The mood suddenly shifted. The air stilled. Desire wound its way through her body, stealthily reminding her it had only gone dormant, not dissipated.

He knelt in front of her. "You handled yourself today like a pro. As always."

She stared at him, her hands wrapped around his

wrists. Her breathing quickened. The smile faded from his lips, and a smoky hunger slid into his eyes.

Then suddenly his mouth was on hers—hot and hungry, full of intense need and power. She moaned and thrust her arms around his neck, parting her legs as she yanked him against her body. He felt incredible at the crux of her thighs. Hard and male pressed against her softness.

An ache pulsed from her center as his kiss seduced and demanded. Her legs shook. Her head swam. She wanted to melt into him, over him. For once, she didn't care about tomorrow. She had to have him. Just once, and maybe this intense ache would go away.

He cupped her butt and pulled her tighter against his erection. Warmth flowed through her body. When he lifted his head to trail kisses along her jaw, she gasped at both the pleasure of his touch and the wild hunger on his face. That desire was for *her*. Not Bambi. Or Barbie. Or Bunny. *Her*.

She slid her fingers through his hair and closed her eyes. "Tony," she breathed.

With that, he stopped. Her eyes popped open.

He raised his head and stared at her. "Ches, I—"

He let go of her as if she'd suddenly caught fire, and, jumping to his feet, he paced across the office. "I can't believe I— I shouldn't have— It was a—"

"It's okay." Francesca rose from the chair, holding her hands out for him to stop. Her knees wobbled a bit, but she stood strong. She wasn't a mistake. She didn't want to hear that word come out of his mouth—true as it was.

"I don't know what's wrong with me."

"Nothing's wrong with you."

He ran his hand through his hair. "Something sure as hell is. You're my best friend, Ches. I can't be doing..." he waved his hand in the direction of the chair "...*that* with you."

"I know. I feel the same way." *Do you? Do you really?* She shook aside her conscience. When he wasn't so close she could remind herself of all that was at stake—a lifetime of trust and friendship, the resort, her heart. She'd seen Tony break dozens—not on purpose, of course. As far as she knew, he'd always been honest with women about his lack of interest in settling down, but she wasn't about to fall into those warm brown eyes of his and never find her way out.

He walked toward her, holding out his hands as if he planned to capture hers, but he obviously thought better of the idea and tucked them into his pockets. "Really? You don't want to..."

"No," she said firmly, as much for her benefit as his. The ache deep in her belly she ignored.

"Last night really screwed us up."

She blew out a breath. "No kidding."

"But we're going to be fine." He angled his head. "Right?"

She smiled with a confidence she didn't even come close to feeling. "Right."

4

DISTANCE. Avoidance. And no physical contact.

The three-part mantra had worked for Tony for a week. He was nearly crazy, but he hadn't had sex with his best friend.

A decent trade-off.

And he finally understood the benefits of hard work. He'd tackled the "to do" lists Francesca had constantly given him with uncharacteristic gusto. He'd personally supervised the filling of the pool, the placement of each and every deck chair, table and potted plant, and had religiously checked the chlorine and pH levels five times a day. He'd gone over the wine inventory—twice—to be sure the stock for the opening weekend dishes was plentiful. He'd even suggested he and Francesca invite some friends for a night to do a trial run with the restaurant, a cooking-class, and a wine tasting. After all, who was better to evaluate their resort than their world-traveling cronies? When she'd encouraged his plan, he'd personally called their friends to invite them and worked with the front-desk manager to assign the rooms.

Then, every night, no matter how tired he was, he'd dragged himself to the bar at Chateau Fontaine. He'd flirted with Barbie—her eyes were green; he'd danced with Misty; he'd bought drinks for Candy, Mandy and

Sandy. To his dismay, not one of them brought about the physical and mental reaction he experienced with Francesca. He compared the hue of their hair and eyes to hers. He compared their intelligence. He compared his sense of ease and comfort. Everyone, every single one was lacking next to Francesca.

But he valiantly kept trying.

So, today, two days before Pierre von Shalburg was due to arrive, and one day before the trial run with his friends, he soaped himself in the shower, looking forward to another night of music, dancing and drinks at the chateau.

You're dreading it, you dummy. At least be a man and admit that to yourself.

"Not on your damn life," he muttered beneath the hot spray.

After he dressed, he exited his room and paused outside Francesca's. Was she in there? If so, what was she doing? Watching TV? Working? Taking a bath?

He groaned and forced himself to continue to the elevator. He was absolutely *not* going there. Not today. Not tomorrow. Not *ever* again.

He was finally getting a handle on this resort manager/responsible business owner thing, and he wasn't about to screw up his bid for respect now. Would Uncle Joe jump his best friend two days before the grand opening of his most ambitious business proposition? No. Absolutely not.

As he entered the cigar bar and nightclub, several people waved. He especially made note of Misty sitting in a booth near the back, a glass of wine in front of her and two women he hadn't met flanking her.

He ordered a vodka martini—dry with olives—then slid onto a stool. "How's business?" he asked Mack, the bartender.

"Better than ever." He slid the drink in front of Tony. "Until you open, that is."

"There's plenty of business to go around."

"I guess. But we won't be seeing much of you after Friday, huh?"

"Probably not." Tony sipped his drink and considered the idea that his social life as he knew it would be coming to an end. That couldn't happen because he had to keep his distance from Francesca. But surely in this business one could mix work and play. Mingle with bathing beauties. Laugh with friends. It was all going to happen—and soon.

"I'll come down now and then to keep tabs on the competition," he said to Mack.

"And to lead all the gorgeous ladies back to your place."

Tony smiled—even modestly he thought. "When you got it..."

Mack laughed, then leaned forward. "Hey, man, take pity on Misty back there. She yakked my ear off for about an hour earlier, wanting the 411 about you."

Tony turned, smiling at the sleek blonde in the back booth. "No kidding?" And why did that idea not cause his heart to pound in anticipation, his mind to whirl with ideas of getting close to the lady in question? *Now, if the lady in question had been Francesca...*

Uh, he'd wrap his arm around her in a friendly hug and invite her to sit next to him.

So he could inhale her sweet fruity scent, smile into

her soft blue eyes. He'd slide his hand from her knee, up her skirt and along her inner thigh. His fingers would stroke her skin. He wanted to sense her heat, the dampness at the juncture of her legs. To tease and heighten her need and pleasure. He'd felt her need the night he'd slid into her bed. Had that really happened by accident? Or had part of him honed in on the woman he truly desired?

He'd kiss the tender spot beneath her ear, the one that made her groan and arch her back as she'd done the other night in the office. His touch affected her; he knew it did.

"Ah, come on, man," Mack said, flinging a towel over his shoulder. "If a woman looked at me like that, I'd leave tire marks getting to her."

Tony blinked. "Huh?"

Mack nodded toward the back of the bar. "Misty." He paused, narrowing his eyes. "Are you sure you feel okay?"

"Oh, yeah. I'm great. I think I'll go see who Misty's friends are."

Mack moved down the bar to fill another customer's order. "I want details."

Tony nodded and picked up his drink, though he didn't think there'd be much to detail.

Oh, yes, there will be. Distance. Avoidance. And no physical contact.

No, no, no. That's the Francesca mantra. What's the Misty mantra?

Go for it.

Now, that's a mantra.

It was easy to shift into charming mode. Not a challenge, of course, but still, he applied himself. Misty and her blond friends—Camy and Ally—loved his stories of worldwide travel, they laughed at his jokes, and they were all available, lovely and interested.

Tony, however, was miserable. He found the pursuit ordinary. He found the women only mildly attractive.

He wanted Ches.

He felt like a flame enclosed in a upside-down glass, struggling to burn within its constraints.

Gulping his drink, he laughed halfheartedly at Misty's recounting of a party on the beach last weekend. What a fraud he was. These women deserved more than a halfhearted charmer who'd lost the will to party.

Then his gaze locked on a woman at the club's entrance. She had a knockout figure and wore a just-above-knee-length black halter dress and wrap-around-the-ankle stilettos. Holy hell. He swallowed, letting his gaze rise slowly to the exquisite woman's face.

Francesca.

Well, damn.

FRANCESCA PAUSED at the entrance to the club. *Humph.* Tony thought *he'd* have all the fun, did he?

Surrounded by three blondes, indeed.

After giving him a quick wave, she rolled her shoulders back, then walked toward the bar. Ignoring her jangling nerves—which had nothing whatsoever to do with Tony looking delicious enough to eat—she slapped down her purse. "I'll have a glass of wine."

A smiling young bartender leaned toward her. "Any particular kind?"

"A...chardonnay." Boy, that sounds adventurous. "A strong one."

The bartender's grin widened. "One strong chardonnay."

Francesca flushed. When she couldn't even properly order a glass of wine, it was a sure sign she'd been working too hard. Which was exactly why she'd come. She'd known it was damn well time to do something for herself. So, she'd pulled her party dress and snazzy shoes out of the back of her closet, and now here she was scoping the place for The One.

Because if he didn't show up soon, she was going to ruin one of the best friendships of her life and screw up her business partnership as well.

Tony had spent the last week ignoring her—which she was frankly grateful for, since resisting him had become an Olympic sport—so she'd spent the time when she wasn't working plowing through the resort's magazines. *Cosmopolitan, Marie Claire* and *Glamour* had all agreed—if you wanted The One, you had to *find* him. You couldn't wait for him to just show up.

The bartender set her wine in front of her, then held out his hand. "I'm Mack, by the way."

Francesca shook his hand. "Francesca D'Arcy."

"Would that be the brilliant, multi-talented Francesca?"

Was he coming on to her? She was flattered, but Mack barely looked old enough to pour drinks legally, and there'd been no bells or whistles or fireworks when she'd first spotted him, so he couldn't be The One. "I, uh—"

"Tony's told me all about you," Mack continued.

"Oh." *Smile, you dummy.* She did, but it seemed forced. She sipped her chardonnay. How did one go about this? Small talk and flirting required practice, and she couldn't remember the last time she'd done either. She wished she could talk to Tony. He was an expert.

Wait. She *could* talk to Tony. He was twenty feet away.

She glanced in his direction. Of course he looked really busy laughing uproariously at whatever the blonde with crooked teeth had just said. Though the teeth were bad, the rest of her was gorgeous, especially those perfect—probably perfectly fake—boobs. Perfect hair. Perfectly dressed. The kind of woman he always went for. Nothing like her.

Quit being goofy. You've gone to Tony for advice about guys dozens of times.

That was before they'd rolled around nearly naked in her bed. And before he'd kissed her senseless in his office nine days, two hours and three minutes ago.

But they were *not* lovers, she told herself. They were not *going* to be lovers. They were friends. Best friends. What was there to be awkward about?

"Hold my spot, Mack," she said as she hitched her purse on her shoulder. "I'll be right back."

"Sure thing."

Francesca approached Tony and his mini-harem. She smiled wanly when the women glared at her.

"May I talk to you a minute?" she said, meeting Tony's gaze.

Tony looked to the woman on his right, who would need to slide from the booth so he could get out.

She laid her hand on his arm and didn't scoot an inch. "Oh, Tony, do you have to go *now*?"

Francesca tapped her foot. "Yes, he does." She wanted to knock out one of those crooked teeth. "I'll bring him back. Don't worry."

Tony patted the blonde's hand. "Francesca's my business partner. Boring, resort-running stuff, you know."

As he scooted out of the booth, Francesca fought to keep her temper on simmer, but as they reached the bar and Tony dropped onto the stool next to her, she found herself grinding her teeth.

"What's up?"

"Boring, resort-running stuff?"

"Come on, Ches. She wouldn't get out of the booth."

"Boring, resort-running stuff?"

"Hey, I'm sorry. Okay?" He accepted a fresh drink from Mack with a nod and a smile. "What are you doing here anyway?"

"I'm taking a break. You take breaks. Aren't I entitled—"

"Of course you are. Man, you're in a bad mood."

"I'm putting in too many hours and not getting enough sleep."

"I'll drink to that." He tapped his glass against hers. "What's wrong?"

I miss you. I don't like this tension between us.

What was wrong at the resort, he'd meant. Of

course. She stared into her wineglass, feeling like a jerk.

"Are you going to tell me what you wanted to talk about?"

She glanced over at him. His normally warm brown eyes reflected wariness. "How do you flirt?"

He choked on his drink. "What?"

"Come on, Tony. You're a pro. I need some tips."

"What for?"

"So I can find The One."

"Who?"

"Mr. Right."

His face paled. "Why would you want to do that?"

"Because he's out there, and if I don't start looking for him, I'm never going to find him." She shrugged. "According to *Cosmo* anyway."

"When did you start reading *Cosmo?*"

"This week. What difference does it make? Are you going to help me or not?"

"No."

"No? Why not?"

"You don't need help. That dress is sending plenty of *I'm available* signals all on its own."

"What's wrong with my dress?"

"Nothing. If you're trying to be obvious."

Francesca gasped. He was one to talk. And beneath her anger, she was hurt. Tony always helped her, and now he'd suddenly refused. "Toddle on back to the Three Blondes, Tony. I think I can handle things from here."

He pushed his drink aside and stood. "Fine, I will."

THE SHARKS were closing in. Four of them. Drooling, smiling, drink-buying sharks.

With Francesca the delicate meal in the middle.

From across the bar, Tony glowered at the group. Misty and the other women had gone off to the hot tub. They'd invited him, but he hadn't wanted to go. And a damn good thing he hadn't, too. Somebody had to watch out for his best friend. Francesca obviously didn't know what went through a man's mind when he saw a woman dressed like her, with a body like hers, laughing provocatively like her.

Not that *he* had those thoughts about her. No, siree. He'd wrangled that pesky attraction into submission. Good thing, too, since he certainly wouldn't be attracted to a woman on a mission to find The One. No way. He wasn't settling down for a very long time. Maybe never. He had a buffet of women to sample from. Why would he want to choose just one?

Damn, man, that attitude's just wrong.

He ignored his conscience, reminding himself this was the part of him that thought resort ownership was a great way to fulfill his life. So far, all he'd done was work himself to exhaustion and pick up an unrelenting attraction to his best friend.

"I wanna know what you're doing down here every night when you've got a babe like that to work with?" Mack asked, his gaze glued to Francesca.

Tony studied his drink—he'd downgraded from a martini to Perrier and regretted that decision. "I'm about to strangle the whole crowd. You want to be next?"

"Do I get to touch her first? Might be worth it."

Tony flicked his gaze in Mack's direction. "Try it."

"Hey, man, just makin' conversation. If I didn't know you better, I might think you were jealous."

"Don't be ridiculous." Tony sipped his drink, his knuckles white as he clutched the glass. "But if that idiot in the *very* poorly cut suit lays his hand on her knee one more time, I'm gonna jerk his tongue out through his ears."

"But you're not jealous."

"No. We're *friends*. Like brother and—" Actually, they were *nothing* like siblings. He'd never known anyone he'd like less as a sister, in fact. "I'm protective of her. She's very sweet and trusting. She doesn't know what those sharks are after."

"She looks like she's holding her own pretty well."

Francesca flipped her hair over her shoulder and sent a warm smile toward Bad Suit Guy.

Tony's left eye twitched.

Then the guy on her right laid his hand on her shoulder.

Tony stood. "I'll be back in a minute, Mack."

Mack simply shook his head.

Tony rounded the bar and approached the group. "Ches, I need to talk to you."

She pulled her gaze away from Shoulder Guy long enough to glare up at him. "Don't I look busy to you, Tony?"

"No."

This time she didn't even bother to look at him. "Go away, Tony."

"No."

Bad Suit Guy rose, crossing his arms over his chest. "I think the lady wants you to leave...Tony."

Tony could actually feel his blood boil. What was wrong with Francesca? Couldn't she see through these guys? Through their fake smiles and empty compliments and bad suits? They weren't good enough for her.

And why wouldn't she talk to him? She'd actually *dismissed* him. She'd never done that. She'd always been supportive, encouraging and...there.

Well, he was *going* to talk to her, dammit, even if he had to beat this jerk to a pulp to do it.

Okay, maybe that wasn't such a bad plan. He took a step forward.

Francesca jumped to her feet, placing her body between him and Bad Suit Guy. "This better not take long," she said, glaring at Tony.

Tony grabbed her arm, and thought about throwing a quick jab at Bad Suit Guy, but he really wanted to keep Francesca on his side and knew she wouldn't approve of violence. He merely smirked at the guy as he walked away.

"I'll be back," Francesca said to the sharks, smiling and waving.

Tony pulled her into a quiet corner and muttered, "What do you think you're—"

"You interrupted my date."

"*That*—" he pointed at the shark pool "—wasn't a date. It was a...*ménage à cinq*."

She poked her finger at his chest. "You have a lot of nerve saying that about *me*. What about *you*?"

He leaned over her, backing her against an unoccupied corner table. The heat of her body collided with his. "I count *four*, Ches. *Four* guys."

Her breath heaved out harsh and fast through her mouth. Her blue eyes shot sparks. "They've all been perfect gentlemen."

Damn, she's sexy as hell. Tony's temples throbbed in time with his erection. He wanted to pin her to the table so she could feel how wildly she affected him. So he could have her. Keep her. Just for him. "Wrong. That guy in the bad suit touched your knee—twice. Then that geek on your right put his hand on your shoulder."

"So *what?* I asked for your help earlier and you refused, remember? Besides they—" Her eyes narrowed. "*You* were watching awfully closely."

"*Somebody* has to look out for you."

She smiled suddenly. "And you just happened to be available?" She laid her hand on his chest and pushed him back, then she peeked around his shoulder. "Where's your harem?"

"Hot tub."

"I see."

Tony's heart pounded. He clenched his hands into fists, but his attempt at control did little good. She smelled incredible. She looked...delicious. Why didn't she ever wear dresses like that around *him?* All *he* got were turtlenecks. "Where did you get that dress anyway? I've never seen you wear it."

"I wore it to your cousin's wedding last year."

He raked his gaze over her. Her bronzed, bare shoulders gleamed in the dim light; the swell of her breasts peeked out from the haltered top of her dress. Even her knees were sexy. How could he have missed all that? He searched his memory for his cousins' weddings— there'd been a lot, so it took him a minute—but he came up blank in the Francesca-as-a-*Playboy* Playmate department. "It's too revealing," he insisted.

Her jaw dropped. "I don't see how it's any of your business what I wear." She whirled away.

He snagged her by the arm and brought her around to face him.

She was breathing hard and scowling. He was all but snarling.

And he suddenly realized he'd been acting a lot more like a jealous lover than a best friend.

"I—" Scared to the bone, he could only stare at her. "I'll see you later."

Then he turned and stalked from the bar.

5

THE NEXT AFTERNOON, Francesca strode by the registration desk, heading toward the revolving door, so she could greet the last two of the friends who'd agreed to participate in the resort's trial run.

Pierre von Shalburg and the rest of their opening-weekend guests would arrive tomorrow. She'd spent the day working with the kitchen staff on menus and cooking demonstrations. Kerry was so thrilled with the opportunity to impress such an influential foodie, he'd come up with some original dishes to serve alongside the wines at the tastings. Carlos—when they could drag him away from mothering the kittens—had perfected Kerry's creations.

Tony had finally absorbed the significance of von Shalburg's opinion and had spent even more time with the sommelier on the wine pairings. Francesca prayed they were ready.

She walked outside as Allison Masters was exiting a limousine. "Francesca!" Her willowy blond friend embraced Francesca, promptly whacking her on the back with her oversized Gucci purse. "Oh, sorry." She stepped back and stumbled.

Francesca caught her by her arm. She had to admire the dedication of anyone as klutzy as Allison who continued to wear four-inch heels.

Robert Summers, Allison's boyfriend since high school and fiancé for the last five years, slid his arm around her waist. "One of these days, you're going to break your ankle in those things."

Allison smiled at him. "Admit it. You like catching me."

Rob kissed her lightly. "You know I do."

This was interesting. Rob and Allison had dated so long, they always seemed like an old married couple, and here they were googling at each other. "You two seem...happy."

"Why wouldn't we be?" Allison asked, eyes wide with innocence.

"No reason." At least *somebody* was okay in the relationship department. This morning Tony had cancelled their usual coffee in the lobby, and Francesca hadn't seen him all day. Their argument and harsh words from last night had left her with a hollow spot in her stomach, and his avoidance only made her feel worse.

Not finding The One last night hadn't helped. She'd enjoyed a light flirtation with the guys from the bar, but the sparks had really been nonexistent. She'd hung out mainly to prove to Tony that he wasn't the only one who had a social life.

Forcing her own problems aside, Francesca gave the valet unloading the bags a smile of encouragement— her staff was ready for this whole thing even if she had the willies—then she directed Rob and Allison into the lobby. "All the rooms on the third floor are suites, so I—"

"Oh, it's lovely." Allison leaned her head back and turned a circle as she stared at the glass ceiling.

Rob, who was the conservative one of their group of friends, had expressed doubts about the resort's possibility of success, but now he smiled widely. "Terrific. The pictures Tony showed me didn't do the place justice."

That's six for six, Francesca thought with a smile. Each and every one of her friends had halted just inside the door and stared in pleased wonder at the greenhouse-like lobby. And these were people who'd traveled the world many times, stayed in so many marbled, red-carpeted hotels they probably couldn't distinguish between them. Bella Luna's distinctive design had had just the effect she'd hoped for.

"Do all the rooms open onto the lobby?" Rob asked.

"Yes, the lobby ceiling is three floors high, and all the rooms wrap around it. That layout allowed us to give each room lots of windows and an exterior balcony overlooking the vineyard."

"It's really great, Francesca," Allison said. "I'm so happy for you."

Francesca gave them a full tour of the first floor, including the cooking-demonstration rooms, the wine-tasting rooms, the gift shop and the restaurant. They ended up at the bar, where she'd dropped off the others who'd been arriving over the last hour.

When she walked inside, though, she noticed Tony still hadn't shown up. Where had he run off to *now*?

She clenched her hands. "You two go ahead. Sonny will make you a drink. I need to make a quick phone call."

As Sonny Compton waved at them from behind the bar, Francesca hurried to the maître d's stand. She wasn't entirely sure why Tony had invited Sonny. They weren't exactly bosom buddies these days. Sonny had always been a practical joker, but that betting pool he'd come up with on how long Tony's foray into business would actually last had moved way over the tacky line. She suspected Tony was, in fact, humiliated by it. Maybe he just wanted to show Sonny how much he'd accomplished.

She'd just punched out Tony's room number on the phone keypad when she heard his voice. "Sorry I'm late, everyone. I had to finish up some paperwork."

She whirled to find him just a few feet away.

As she set the phone in its cradle, he turned toward her, his brow furrowed as if he hadn't noticed her standing there.

They exchanged a long, silent look. She ignored her racing heart, the way her hands went damp as she absorbed the sight of him in black slacks and a black silk shirt. He seemed tall, dark...dangerous. And distant.

"It's four-thirty, old boy," Sonny said, glancing at his watch. "Putting in some long hours, aren't we?"

Tony walked toward the bar, which Sonny had taken charge of the moment he'd arrived. "You know how it is with us working stiffs."

Smiling, Sonny winked. "No, pal, I don't think I do."

Tony glared at Sonny and said nothing. No smile. No smart comeback.

Francesca noted thankfully that Allison filled the awkward silence by throwing her arms around Tony's stiff body. She gave him a smacking kiss on his cheek, leaving a bright-red lipstick print on his skin. "This place is so great! Do we get to do the cooking classes and wine tastings like real guests?"

Finally, Tony's charming smile appeared. "Of course, and you *are* real guests."

Francesca kept her gaze glued to him. Was she the only one who noticed the forced edge to his smile? The way darkness lingered in his eyes?

Sonny clapped. "Okay, people, on to the important stuff. Drinks. Who needs a refill? Rob, Allison, Tony, Ches, what do you want?"

Rob and Allison gave their orders, then wandered down the bar to talk with the rest of their friends.

"Ches, what about you?" Sonny asked as he tossed ice into glasses.

Francesca slid onto a stool. "How about a glass of w—"

"Where are the bartenders?" Tony asked, his tone impatient.

Over her shoulder, Francesca glared at him.

"Here," Sonny said, sounding confused.

Tony waved his hand. "No, no, I mean our *real* bartenders." He cut his gaze to Francesca. "The ones we pay."

"They'll be here later."

"Why aren't they here now? I thought this was supposed to be a practice run."

"Because the jazz band won't be here till later, and I figured it would be easier to have them all 'practice' at once. And I knew Sonny wouldn't mind tending. I thought an intimate party with our friends would be fun."

"That doesn't seem very responsible."

Francesca's eyes popped wide. "Okay, let's talk." She grabbed Tony by his arm, slid off her stool, then led him out to the lobby. "Not very *responsible?*"

Tony crossed his arms over his chest. "How do we know the guys we've hired can handle the job?"

"Because they have twenty years of bartending experience between them. Somehow, I don't think missing an eight-person cocktail hour will affect their training too adversely."

He leaned close to her face, anger flaring in his eyes. "The last time I checked *I* owned sixty percent of this place, while *you* own ten. *Somehow,* I think you should have talked to me before making this decision."

Shocked, Francesca stepped back. Maybe she should have consulted Tony, but it had, in fact, never occurred to her. And she was so hurt by the way he'd so succinctly put her in her place, she didn't know how to respond. "I—" She rubbed her temples. "I can't believe we're having this fight. We open tomorrow, and our closest friends are twenty feet away, ready to celebrate our success."

"Maybe I don't have a fancy business degree, but I'm doing my best. I'm tired of people treating me like I'm some kind of liability around here."

"I don't treat you that way."

"Yes, you do."

Some part of her realized Tony's feelings had been building a long time, and she knew what had brought them to the fore. Rejection. By her. Before her, by a lot of people. His parents had ignored him for most of his life, pushing him off on nannies and housekeepers.

Uncle Joe was the only one who'd taken a real interest in him, spent time with him and taught him about the vineyards.

Now the people he cared about most—his friends and Joe—were here to witness the risk he'd taken. And he was worried they'd find his efforts lacking.

His friends wouldn't mean to, of course, they just really didn't understand Tony's sudden change of heart. He had money, women and charm. Why would he want to piss all that away working as hard as a resort manager had to work?

And then there was Joe. All he had to do was glance at his nephew with the slightest hint of disappointment. It would crush Tony. And—

Wait just a damn second. How dare he—Mr. Run-Off-to-the-Chateau-Anytime-He-Liked—question her judgment and sense of responsibility? "*My* dedication to this resort has never been in question." She stepped close to him, her gaze drilling into his. "You can swagger in here, play around at owning a fancy resort, impress your friends and your uncle. Bully for you. But I can't just wander back to my bottomless trust fund. I scraped together everything I could to invest in this place. Borrowed money from my parents. This *has* to work for me. And if you don't like the way I do things, you need to tell me *now*."

He glared at her, his breath heaving, his brown eyes dark with anger. "I just want you to tell me what's going on."

"Well, if you were *here* instead of out partying, you might *know* what's going on."

"I am here. I've only gone out at night. And I don't go out at night to avoid work. I go out to avoid *you*."

She blinked. "Me? Why—" *Ding*. The bell of understanding suddenly chimed. He went out for the same reason she had gone out last night. He wasn't looking for The One, of course, but maybe he was looking for someone so he wouldn't be tempted by her.

Maybe that kiss in his office hadn't just been an impulsive, forgotten-the-next-moment thing. Maybe he really had been jealous last night. Ridiculously, she went hot all over at the thought.

He raked his hand through his hair. "Just look at last night. I could have been in the hot tub with Misty and the others, but—"

"Is she the one with crooked teeth?"

He frowned. "She's a busty blonde."

"With crooked teeth."

"Yeah? Well, at least she wasn't wearing a cheap suit that looked as if a cross-eyed tailor had fitted it on an off day."

"Hmm. That was Brad." After years of friendship with Tony she could recognize a bad suit when she saw one. Still, he'd been cute.

"*Brad?* Why am I not surprised? He looked like a Brad—all puffed up with himself, but still managing to drool down your dress."

Francesca smiled. "You're doing it again. Actually, *we're* doing it again." She'd spent a lot of years denying her attraction to Tony, trying to ignore the sinking feeling in her stomach every time she saw him with a new woman, but there didn't seem any point in denial any longer. She drew a deep breath. "I wanted to punch out Miss Crooked Teeth."

He gave her a half smile. "No kidding?"

"No kidding."

"Bad-Suit Brad should feel fortunate he continues to walk upright."

"Really?"

"Really."

She let the rushing pleasure of his warm gaze flow through her for a minute—then she realized, even with their attraction out in the open, their friendship and business partnership was still very much on shaky ground. "What are we going to do?"

He grabbed her hand, yanking her against him. "Let's just do it."

"Do it?"

His gaze locked with hers, he nodded. "One night only. We'll satisfy our curiosity—or whatever brought this on—then we can get on with our lives."

That plan sounded way too simple to resolve all the feelings running riot through her body. "Sex will mess up our friendship."

"We can't go on like this either—arguing, avoiding each other."

She recalled the night she'd woken to find him in her bed, the night he'd kissed her in his office. She wanted that passion again. She wanted to tingle. She wanted her head to swim. She wanted that achy need to invade her blood, so that nothing and no one existed but him. She wanted him. How much she might be willing to sacrifice to have that happen she wasn't sure.

"I don't know," she said. "I need some time to think."

"A challenge?" Stroking his hands across the span of her lower back, he smiled. "I bet I can help you decide."

The last thing she needed was Tony's formidable powers of seduction focused on her while she tried to make a rational decision. "No, Tony—"

"You'll see it my way, I'm sure." He kissed the tender spot beneath her ear.

Her stomach trembled. "Oh, I—" She forced herself to lean back. "We have stuff to settle first. I treat you like a liability, remember?"

He ran his tongue across her earlobe. "No."

Weak, she closed her eyes and angled her head as his fabulous mouth caressed her skin. "Tony, please," she breathed, though she wasn't quite sure whether she was pleading for him to stop or to keep going.

He pulled her tighter against his body. His erection pressed against her stomach. "Mmm. I like the sound of that."

Well aware of how weak she was where he was concerned, she fought desperately for some sense of balance. "I guess this means you're through brooding."

"Oh, yeah."

"And you're not worried about the opening, or Sonny and the rest of our friends?"

"No."

"Hey, what are you two doing?" Sonny called. "You're missing the party."

Tony ignored Sonny. Instead, he inhaled Francesca's spicy, fruity scent.

She tried to push her way out of his arms, but he held on tighter. "We'll be there in a minute," Tony called, then brushed his lips across her delectable throat. Her skin was soft, smooth...delicious.

"Cut it out. Sonny will think we're—"

"Crazy? Beyond reason?" He raised his head, kissing the tip of her nose, and he very nearly drowned in her desire-filled deep-blue eyes. "Too late." He glanced in Sonny's direction. Their friend was staring at them and frowning. "It is our party. I guess we should join it."

Francesca nodded, but her fingers flexed against the front of his shirt. "Probably."

With a sigh, Tony slid his arm across her shoulders and started toward the bar entrance. His fingers quickly became warm against her skin, bared by the one-shoulder, shimmery silver dress she wore. Silvery stockings and matching stilettos made her look like a New Year's Eve sparkler, and the danger of being burned only enticed him further.

She wrapped her arm around his waist and squeezed. He liked the sense of her tucked by his side. His world had been completely off-kilter ever since they'd argued last night. "We've accomplished a lot, you know," she said. "Together."

"When I wasn't running off to the Chateau's bar."

"You've worked as hard as I have," she insisted.

"Think it'll last?"

She looked away. "If you want it to."

He wanted it to. He just wasn't sure he had the drive to be successful. Could he really commit himself the way Joe did?

"Hell, man," Sonny began, shaking his head, "if I'd known being a businessman involved necking in hotel lobbies, I might've tried it years ago." He waggled his eyebrows. "Especially if the chick is Francesca."

Tony stiffened. Francesca wasn't a *chick*, and Sonny better keep his hands off her.

She laughed and linked arms with Sonny.

What's wrong with me? Tony set his jaw against the urge to shove Sonny away from Francesca. He wasn't the jealous type. After all, he didn't want a woman telling him how he could spend his time and with whom, so how could he ask for exclusivity from her?

But then he and Francesca's relationship was very different from any other in his life. Their friendship was an intimate club of two that none of their other friends, no matter how special, could join. And now that special relationship was mixed up with all these other feelings of possession, lust, confusion, more lust.

One night only. If she'd agree, that was the solution to getting himself back to normal. She'd told him she wanted The One, so that plan would work well for her, too. Unlike Francesca, he wasn't worried about their friendship. He'd slept with other women and remained friends afterward. He and Francesca could do that as well.

Distance, avoidance and no physical contact certainly hadn't worked. *Something* had to. He had to resolve this craving in his gut.

As they entered the bar, Allison toasted them with her martini glass. "No work tonight, you two. Come have a drink." She smiled widely. Allison could inhale alcohol vapors and get tipsy, so she and her half-full glass would no doubt make things interesting.

Everyone looked as though they were having a great time, and Tony realized how much he'd missed his friends. With him working and living out on Long Island while most of them lived in Manhattan, they hadn't gotten together often.

Sonny grabbed his elbow as Francesca walked ahead of them. "Anything going on you wanna tell me about, buddy?"

"We open tomorrow, Sonny. There's plenty going on."

His friend raised his eyebrows. "I'm not talking about the resort."

Tony had figured that. He'd just been hoping Sonny would let what he'd witnessed between him and Francesca drop quietly. No such luck. "Nothing's going on between me and Francesca." At least not yet.

"Didn't look that way from where I was standing."

Tony was admitting nothing. "You planning to start another pool?"

Stroking his chin, Sonny rocked back on his heels. "Maybe."

Height had its advantages, and Tony used his to glare down at the not-quite-six-feet Sonny.

"Hey, man, I'm just messin' with you. None of my business." He angled his head, considering. "It's not as crazy as it seems though—you and Ches. You kind of balance each other."

Tony supposed they did, in a way, but he wasn't taking the thought deeper than that. "I need a drink."

Sonny clapped him on the shoulder. "Now you're talkin'."

They joined the others. Altogether they made a party of eight—five men and three women.

Tony downed his martini quickly and didn't protest when Sonny mixed him another. He'd drunk very little the last several days—brooding and alcohol did not mix—so he found himself somewhat lightheaded when he rose from his stool to lead everyone into the restaurant for dinner.

Good. Maybe that would give him courage. Convincing Francesca to sleep with him wouldn't be easy. Once she'd turned the idea around that practical brain of hers, she was likely to come up with a logical reason why his plan wouldn't work. He needed to overwhelm her senses, remind her of the heat they generated.

Courage? He nearly stumbled. He needed *courage* for seduction?

Not in this lifetime.

All he needed was an opportunity. And even that he could create, if need be.

The tuxedoed maître d' was an elegant presence at the entrance to the restaurant, aptly named Anthony's.

Sonny laughed. "Subtle. That's our Tony."

During the lively discussion Tony maneuvered himself next to Francesca, so when they sat she was at his right. *Smoothly done, if I do say so myself,* he thought with a smile as he slid his hand over Francesca's and squeezed briefly.

Her gaze met his over their menus. "Stop. I'm nervous enough."

"Everything's going great, *bella*. What's to be nervous about?"

"I'm not nervous about the resort."

He leaned closer, until their faces were just inches apart. Her eyes widened at his proximity. "What then? You're always thinking about business."

Her face flushed, and Tony felt the answering reaction in his groin. "Not always."

Beneath the table, he trickled his fingers along the inside of her stocking-clad knee. "What are you thinking about?"

She looked up at him through her lashes. "You know."

Opportunity rapped at the door. "Have I told you how beautiful you are tonight?"

"No."

"You are." He slid his fingers up her thigh. She trembled. He smiled. "Have you made your decision yet?"

She grasped his seeking hand, held it still. "I haven't had time."

"Is that what you want? Time?"

"Yes."

He switched his grip on her hand, so he had her own hand gliding up and down on her thigh. "How do you expect me to resist this?"

"We can't do this now."

He glanced down the length of the table. Everyone was looking through their menus, discussing their selections. "No one's paying any attention to us."

"Don't you think *we* should be paying attention to *them*?"

Hmm...probably. This was what he'd been waiting

for—elegant dinners, excellent wines, socializing with friends. But he couldn't focus on anything but Francesca.

Reluctantly, he moved his hand back to the table. Relief danced across Francesca's eyes, and he vowed to see that the desire returned. And soon.

Deciding to re-energize his seduction plans after dinner, he concentrated on what he did best—playing host. He let the restaurant's sommelier reiterate the menu's wine recommendations—the ones they'd worked so hard on together—and gave the young man an encouraging smile when he finished. He ordered a sampling of appetizers for everyone to share and was pleased with his staff's level of service and the quality of the food.

The conversation rolled easily between summer plans and family news until Rob stood, tapping on the side of his wineglass with a fork. "I have an announcement to make." He smiled down at Allison. "Allison and I are getting married."

Confused, everybody stared up at him. Finally, Sonny pointed out, "You've been about to get married for five years, Rob. That isn't news."

Rob pulled Allison up to stand beside him. He gazed at her with a devotion that Tony hadn't seen from him in a long time. "No, we're really getting married. September first."

"Of which year?" Sonny called out.

Allison threw her napkin at him. "This one, dummy."

Smiling, Francesca rose and hugged them. "It's about damn time."

Everyone embraced the couple in turn, and Tony called for champagne. He even offered the first toast.

Inside, though, he felt off-kilter. Rob had told Tony many times that though he loved Allison, he didn't know if his feelings were lifelong. *How do you really know?* he'd asked on many occasions, and Tony had often doubted Rob and Allison would ever take the plunge.

Now Rob was finally getting on with his life. He'd made a decision. He was following through on his commitments.

Maybe it wasn't so far-fetched that Tony could do the same. He could make a success of the resort, proving to Joe that he hadn't misplaced his faith and confidence. Maybe he could even find a wife himself. Someday. Far in the future.

As they finished dessert and champagne, Tony shook off plans for anything beyond Francesca in his bed. He'd figure out the rest of his life later.

He asked their waiter to bring Kerry and Chef Carlos to the table. From the quality of the meal, he figured the kitchen staff had found a way to work well together, despite their conflicts early last week, and he wanted to give them their chance to shine.

Then he directed his attention to Francesca. She was cutting her turtle cheesecake. Dessert equaled the end of dinner. The beginning of seduction.

He laid his arm across the back of her chair, his hand brushing her bare shoulder. He moved with casual ease. He didn't want her nervous. He wanted her loose and hot and wanting him.

She had great shoulders—smooth, golden skin, sleek

muscles. As he watched her close her mouth around a bite of cheesecake, he...well, he wanted to be that cheesecake, but he also realized he liked her profile. The curve of her lips, the angle of her jaw. It amazed him he'd never taken the time to really notice these details before. He'd always thought of her as warm, beautiful and bright, but he'd never before felt this intense need to be with her, touch her.

He couldn't get enough of her. He wanted to breathe in her scent, hold her, absorb her.

Kerry approached the table before he could do much more than consider how he was going to accomplish that. "Ms. D'Arcy, Mr. Galini, how was everything?"

Francesca smiled up at him. "Wonderful, Kerry. You guys did a great job."

"Where's Chef Carlos?" Tony asked, noting the moody chef was nowhere to be seen.

Kerry leaned close. "He's feeding our other... guests."

Ah, the cat family.

Francesca paled. "Not in the kitchen, I hope."

"No, he's keeping them in the gardener's shed like you asked."

Tony smiled sardonically. "At least we don't have to worry about the health inspector."

Then the lights went out.

6

"OH GOD. Not again," Francesca groaned.

"Sit tight," Tony said, squeezing Francesca's arm. "I'll get the flashlight."

"Do you know where it is?"

"In my office."

"That's too far to go in the dark."

"There's one in the kitchen," Kerry put in. "I'll show you."

"No, Kerry, you sit here. I'll go." Pushing back her chair and trying not to let panic choke her, Francesca rose. Now that her eyes had adjusted, she could just make out shapes around her. They had emergency lighting in the halls and above the exits, so some of that filtered into the room.

"You forget to pay the power bill, buddy?" Sonny asked from the other end of the table.

"Ha, ha," Tony said. "Everybody stay put. Francesca and I are going to get a flashlight and candles."

He wrapped his arm around her waist, presumably so they wouldn't lose each other, but his touch had the added effect of shooting off her already frayed nerves like rockets.

How many times had she wished Tony would notice her? Flirt with her? *Gulp.* Seduce her?

And now he'd said he had every intention of doing

just that, and she'd told him she needed to think about it?

As soon as she could see a wall again, she was going to bang her head against it.

Moving slowly, Tony led her away from the table. His pant leg brushed her thigh. She suppressed a moan.

"While you're at it," Sonny cheerily called from behind them, "you might want to think about permanently leaving candles on the tables. Looks like they might come in handy."

Even as Tony tensed, Francesca said, "Ignore him."

Allison's voice also floated out of the darkness. "Oh, be quiet, Sonny."

"Hey, I was just kidding..."

Their voices faded as Francesca and Tony inched across the restaurant, heading toward the kitchen.

"Candles on the tables would have been better," Tony said.

"No. You made the right decision. The individually-controlled track lighting is more intimate. People can make it as bright or dim as they want. Plus, you don't have to worry about waiters toting around lighters and guests catching themselves on fire. Once we get this problem with the power company resolved, we'll be fine."

"My personal cheerleader?" he said after a moment's pause.

"Ra, ra, ra."

He pulled her to a stop, then slid his arms around her from behind. "Speaking of intimacy..."

Her heart punched her ribs. "Uh-huh?"

"It's kind of interesting—" his hand glided down the curve of her hip "—feeling our way through the dark." He brushed her hair to the side, kissing the base of her neck. "Remind you of anything you'd like to do?"

Francesca's head swam as his scent and heat washed over her. "Yeah. Throttle the power company."

He rested his chin on her shoulder. "You're not making this easy."

"I'm not supposed to. *You're* the predatory male, pursuing and seducing vulnerable, little female me."

"Are you going to let me?"

"Damned if I know."

He pressed his mouth beneath her ear. "I know."

Her stomach tilted, desire crawling deep into her body. Her attempt at lightness and diversion was obviously a bust. "We should really get that flashlight."

"Later." He grabbed her hand and pulled her into the kitchen, the door swinging shut behind them.

The emergency lighting had kicked on, so she could see the intent, predatory gleam in his eyes.

Half smiling, he stalked forward, backing her against the counter. The bronzed column of his throat brushed the tip of her nose. "I've waited way too long for this."

She swallowed as he lowered his head.

Cupping her jaw in his hand, he drew her close and captured her lips with his. He wasted no time on subtleties, sliding his tongue past her lips, caressing, seducing. She dug her fingers into his silk shirt. Trembling weakness suffused her. But she held on.

With the hard length of his body against hers, her

hips couldn't resist jerking forward to bump his hardness, and a moan escaped her lips.

His hand pressed against the small of her back, molding her to him as he trailed kisses down her cheek, then her throat. He nipped at her skin, his teeth scraping lightly, enticingly, his breath rushing over her, hot and labored.

Raising her hand to thread her fingers through the soft, thick hair at his temple, she dropped her head back. "This is crazy. We have to get the candles."

"I can see just fine."

She drew a shuddering breath as he ran his tongue along the edge of her dress, dipping beneath the fabric to stroke the top of her breast. "The others."

"There's nobody in here but us." He flicked his tongue across her earlobe. "Finally. Thank God."

Again, his mouth sank against hers. He drank from her; he gave to her. All the while, her head reeled. She'd suspected that being the focus of his attention would be exciting, but she really had no idea how intense the whole experience would be.

Bracing his hands against her hips, he pulled her tight against his body. His heart pounded. His erection pulsed. "Please, *bella.*"

The raw need in his voice scraped across her heightened senses. Please *what?* They should be getting the candles, tending to their guests and figuring out why the power had gone off, but she could hardly think straight, much less figure out either his or the power company's motives.

"I need you," he breathed against her throat.

Well, hell. How was she supposed to resist *that?* After so many years of suppressed lust she was trying—really—to make a rational, logical, all-thought-out decision about taking the next step. But when the potential lover-in-question continually—

He cupped her breasts, gliding his thumbs across them. Even through the fabric of her dress her nipples hardened, pulsed.

Continually did stuff like *that*...

Suddenly, he straightened. He slid his hands up her back, holding her tight against his chest. His heart hammered against her cheek. "We have to get the candles."

She closed her eyes against reality, savoring the sensation of his silk shirt teasing her skin. "We do?"

He sighed. "Yeah." As he looked down at her, his eyes narrowed. "You're trembling."

Duh? "Really?"

He grasped her elbow. "Yes. Are you okay?"

Definitely not. "I'm—"

He smiled then, distracting her. "I did that, didn't I?"

"I have no idea what you're talking about."

"Yes, you do." His grin widened. "You want me. You didn't want me to stop."

She flipped her hair over her shoulder. "I told you earlier we needed to think about the others, but you didn't want to listen."

"I still don't. But I'm learning I should. From you, actually."

She hoped her shock didn't show too blatantly. Good God, Tony really was becoming responsible.

"Don't worry. I'll start again, *bella*." He stroked the

back of his hand down her face. "In fact, I can't wait. Can you?"

Her gaze jumped to his. She shook her head.

Smiling and letting go, he stepped back. She shivered at the loss of his heat, but she focused on his face. His skin was flushed, and his eyes reflected hunger—hunger for *her*—but just for a moment, then he banked his feelings and moved away.

She fought to regain her balance. She thought of the times in the past she'd maneuvered situations so that she could be with him, whether it was canceling a date or rearranging her schedule to accommodate his. None of that had seemed to make a difference. Yet, after a few minutes of groping he was desperate to have her. The instability of a relationship built on that gave her the willies. But then this wasn't a relationship.

One night only.

He opened a drawer. "Flashlight?"

"To the right of the stovetop."

Once he'd found the light and flipped it on, Francesca crossed to the phone on the wall. "There are some candles in the pantry," she said to Tony over her shoulder as she dialed information.

Once she was connected to the power company, she pressed buttons in response to the automated instructions, and after being cut off only twice—probably a record for them—she finally got to leave a message to report her outage. *Oh, yeah*, she thought, *that's some emergency number.*

She tried not to panic. Her reputation as a businesswoman was riding on this venture. She didn't want to flip out over something so minor as the power going off. Minor? Ha! Electricity had ceased to be a minor concern at least a hundred years ago.

Tony drew his finger across her bare shoulder. "Relax, *bella*. You, me, candlelight, music, dancing. It's not so bad, huh?"

She grabbed his arm. "Music. How's the band going to play? Microphones and speakers need electricity. The back-up generators are only for the food."

Tony set aside the flashlight and box of candles. He laid his hands on her shoulders, turning her to face him. "It'll be fine. We'll all sit close to the band. They won't need microphones."

She shook her head. "It's so unprofessional. What will they think? What if this happens tomorrow night when Pierre von Shalburg is here?"

He smiled. "It won't. We'll talk to the power company first thing in the morning. We'll get everything straightened out." He squeezed her shoulders. "This is just a bump in the road."

"How can you be so calm?" she asked, exasperated with herself and the whole situation.

"I'm not a worrier."

"Why?"

"It's pointless." He tucked the box of candles beneath his arm and flipped on the flashlight. "Come on."

They'd only gone a few steps when she remembered the chef. "Good grief, Chef Carlos is out in the gardener's shed."

"I'll go get him." Tony handed her the box of candles, then lit one for her. He started toward the back door with the flashlight.

Trying to set aside the troubling ache in her stomach, Francesca turned in the opposite direction. She wasn't going to panic about this. Everything was going to be fine.

"Ches?" Tony called softly.

She turned, only able to see the outline of his body in the back doorway. "Yeah?"

"Do you have an answer for me yet?"

She swallowed. Her body said one thing, her brain something entirely different. "No."

"I guess I'll just have to keeping trying to convince you."

Desire rolled through her body. "I guess so."

"I'm looking forward to it," he said, then he was gone.

Francesca blew out a breath. "You and me both," she whispered to herself.

She shook off a shiver of anticipation and headed back to her guests. They had all taken the power outage in stride and were looking forward to hearing the band and dancing till dawn. Francesca was grateful for their positive attitudes, but knew the guests who were to arrive in less than twenty-four hours wouldn't be nearly so understanding.

Unless the entire Northeast had blacked out again, she must have missed a detail, something about the billing maybe—that was the only explanation for this fiasco. This *thing* with Tony had her troubled and distracted. She'd been handed her dream of business ownership on a silver platter, and she was screwing it up with raging hormones.

It was so unlike her, she didn't know whether to laugh or cry.

Worse still, she was less and less sure she could resist taking another disastrous step closer to him. Just look at her behavior in the kitchen. When he touched her, she lost all sense of time and place. She could only think about him, her need for him, his effect on her senses.

Would trying to resist their attraction distract her more than giving in?

Hell, if I know.

After finding the band hanging out in the dark lobby, she led the group into the bar. Everyone helped set the candles around the room, and the light dancing off the walls added to the relaxed and intimate atmosphere. The musicians were very cool about the lack of power and told her they could get by with percussion and horns. Allison and Rob discussed reception dates and rates with them. Maybe, *maybe*, her reputation as a hotel owner wouldn't explode in her face before it even officially began.

She'd settled herself at the bar with a glass of champagne and had actually begun to relax when Tony entered with Chef Carlos. The chef, naturally, was scowling.

Allison grabbed Francesca's forearm. "Oh, my God. Ches, that's—"

"My chef."

"But he looks like—"

"I know. Don't mention it. He's very sensitive about the whole thing. Tell him you liked the pasta primavera." She waved them over. "Chef Carlos, what a wonderful meal. Top-notch as always."

Chef Carlos's scowl deepened. "I can't make my art, Ms. D'Arcy, without my ovens."

Tony smiled with way more confidence than Francesca herself felt—but then she'd dealt with the power company once already. "We'll get everything straightened out in the morning," he said.

"My pasta primavera was just divine," Allison said, gazing in awe at Chef Carlos.

"Chef, how about a drink?" Tony added, waving the bartender over.

The taciturn man's expression softened a bit. From the offer of alcohol or from the compliments, Francesca wasn't sure. And, frankly, she didn't care. She didn't know how much more she could take tonight. Her sensual nerves were on edge; her professional confidence shaken.

Five minutes later Chef Carlos was surrounded by admirers. Francesca thought she saw a smile briefly appear on his face—though that just as easily could have been a trick of the flickering candlelight.

A minuscule bit of tension eased from her shoulders. Then Tony whispered in her ear. "We throw a pretty good party."

His warm breath tickled her neck, igniting her blood. His chest brushed her back, and she couldn't help but imagine unbuttoning his shirt, parting the black silk and sliding her palm across his warm skin and hard muscles. The sweet, hot scent that clung to him would envelop her senses, making her head spin, her muscles go lax. He'd drawn her into his spell long ago, and she doubted anything could help her escape now.

When she turned, she looked up into his eyes. And forgot how to breathe.

Tony flexed his hand against Francesca's waist and stared at her as if he'd never seen her before.

How was it he'd spent most of his life with her but hadn't noticed how bright and sexy her eyes were? How curvy and sensuous her body had become? He'd always admired her intelligence and loyalty to her friends, but suddenly he felt a connection with her he couldn't dismiss or handle smoothly. He'd fallen into the wrong bed, and now his world revolved around her.

It was enough to give a committed playboy nightmares.

And fantasies.

"Dance with me," he murmured in her ear, inhaling the seductive, spicy scent clinging to her skin. He pulled her against him and had to hold back a groan when her slinky, soft body pressed against the need pulsing through his muscles.

"I—" She stared up at him, her blue eyes bright with desire.

"Come on, Ches. Please."

She simply nodded.

On the dance floor, Tony let the low moan of the saxophone wind its way around his senses. Candlelight flickered across Francesca's golden skin, exaggerating the darkly romantic mood. Closing his eyes, he savored the sensation of simply touching her.

She slid her hands up his chest, pausing slightly as her thumb brushed one of his shirt buttons.

His heart raced in response. He pulled her closer, so her hips brushed against his, knowing she had to feel his desire for her, this damnable hunger that wouldn't abate. Part of him was very afraid one night wouldn't be enough, that no amount of time would ever satisfy him.

His body refused to care about this possibility, though. It just wanted to sink into her softness and drive away this clawing need.

He stared down at her, willing her to raise her head and meet his gaze. He needed to assure himself he wasn't alone, that she wanted him as much as he wanted her.

He slid his hands up and down her spine, relishing the sensation as the material of her dress gave way to soft, smooth skin.

Was she that silky all over? Which areas of her body were the softest? The most sensitive?

What rhythm would he set when he finally made love to her? Would he be so anxious to have her that he'd be unable to find his usual finesse? Would there be tenderness, or just an all-out, blinding push to completion? When she climaxed would she moan? Or scream?

The possibilities rolled through his mind like a gathering storm, stretching his nerves taut, turning his gut to Jell-O.

Finally, her gaze flicked to his. Her eyes were dark and smoky, her pupils dilated. Looking at him as if he was the main course at a banquet, she licked her lips, and he nearly moaned aloud.

"I want you so much I can't see straight," he said.

She slid her hands around his neck, her fingertips brushing the hair at his nape. "This is crazy, Tony. We have a business to run." She searched his gaze as if he could give her the answers she needed. "We can't act this way."

"I don't see why not."

"The resort—"

"Will still be here. I'm not planning to make out in the lobby in front of the guests." He smiled. "Though that big round bench near the ivy trellis has possibilities."

"Be serious."

"I am." Not breaking her stare, he angled his head. "I've never been more serious in my life. I want you. I *have* to have you."

Her eyes widened, then narrowed. "Okay, that's just not normal. *Especially* for you.".

"Doesn't seem to matter. It's there."

"Why, Tony? Why, after all this time?"

He shrugged. "Why not?"

She shook her head, and tendrils of her dark hair slid across her shoulders. "You've got to do better than that."

He didn't know how he could put his feelings into words, wasn't sure he *wanted* to. "I guess it was seeing you in that silky pink thing the other night. I can't seem to get that picture out of my head."

"Mmm. I've got some pretty vivid pictures running around my head, too."

He leaned toward her, pressing his lips softly to her ear. "See anything you can't resist exploring?"

"It all looks pretty interesting."

He groaned. "I know the feeling."

"Would you have kissed me that night if you'd been awake?"

Yikes. Honesty or a half truth to further seduction?

This is Francesca, he reminded himself. If nothing else was to come of this sudden attraction to each other, they could at least maintain their honesty. "No. There was a line of friendship there I don't think I would have crossed, though I guess part of me must have been attracted to you for some time. Why else would my reaction have been so...strong?" *Aching, pulsing, hard-as-a-rock, to be precise.*

"Are you sorry it happened?"

"I was at first. Our friendship means everything to me, Ches. I didn't want anything to mess that up."

"And now?"

"Now it's like every day I'm seeing you for the first time." He trailed his fingers across her shoulder. "I never realized how silky and golden your skin was. I never noticed how your eyes go smoky when you're aroused."

"Are they smoky now?" she asked in a whisper, her gaze locked with his.

"Oh, yeah." He cupped her jaw in his palm. "I can't stop myself from noticing everything about you, and I can't let go of these feelings. I can't make them go away."

"But you tried."

"Didn't you? Aren't you still?" He smiled as she

nodded. "You're my best friend. You always will be. But I'm past able to go back to the way things were. We have to go forward."

She said nothing for several long moments, then, "Maybe we do."

Tony's blood pressure shot through the roof. "Is that a yes?"

"I don't know, I—"

"Hey, man, you're hogging her," Sonny said, cutting in. He turned Francesca in a circle. "My turn."

Tony clenched his fists. His body throbbed with need for her, and the level to which he was actually tempted to punch out one of his closest friends forced him to take a long step back.

Later, Francesca mouthed over Sonny's shoulder.

Tony's heart jumped. *What* later? They'd talk? They'd negotiate? They'd get naked and horizontal?

All interesting possibilities. He wondered what the chances were of getting rid of an entire jazz band and his closest friends in the next three minutes.

He forced himself to head back to the bar. He spoke to Allison, Rob and Chef Carlos. What he said, he had no idea. He drank something—Perrier, vodka or motor oil. Maybe all three.

Friends, lovers. They could be both. He'd been friends with other lovers. Why should this be any different?

But then everything about his relationship with Francesca was different.

He glanced at the dance floor where she and Sonny were dancing, and ignored a feeling that some would call jealousy.

Yeah, different.

For the rest of the night—the only highlight of which was the lights mysteriously blinking back on around ten-thirty—he went through the motions. He pretended to be genuinely amused at Sonny's jokes. He pretended interest in Allison and Rob's wedding plans. No one except Francesca seemed to notice his distraction.

By clenching his jaw and keeping his hands wrapped around his glass, he managed to keep his hands off her. Afraid he wouldn't be able to let her go, he didn't ask her to dance again.

The night dragged on and on and on. What was *with* these people? Were they going to party till dawn? Through lunch tomorrow?

At one-fifteen he yawned and stretched. "Man, I'm beat."

Dead silence followed this announcement.

Rob and Sonny exchanged a puzzled glance.

"Are you sure you're feeling okay?" Allison asked.

"Fine," he said. "Just tired. I think I'll head up to bed."

"Tired?" Sonny echoed.

"Bed?" Rob asked. *"Alone?"*

Allison laid her hand across his forehead. "I think he's got a fever."

Francesca met his gaze and covered her mouth with her hand to stifle a laugh.

Talk about overreacting. He wasn't *always* the last one to leave a party. Maybe next to last.

Disgusted, Tony jumped off his stool. He'd had it— with his friends, this party and most especially himself.

He didn't know this moody, scowling person he'd become.

All over a woman. Even if she was a remarkable woman.

"I've got to get up early. Good night," he said, spinning on his heel.

"Come on, man. Don't go," Sonny called after him.

"I'll see you at breakfast," Tony said without turning around. "Have fun."

Since he was anything but tired, he headed through the lobby to the pool. Maybe the fresh air would clear his head. The lights had come on via a timer, throwing the deck into pools of light and giving the water a ghostly blue glow.

He sank onto one of the deck loungers, stretching his legs out in front of him. It was a pity party for one, and he was damn glad that was so. He was embarrassed to have anyone see him like this.

So, of course, that's how Francesca found him a few minutes later.

"I'm not very good company right now," he said, not glancing up at her.

She sat next to him, her hip brushing his thigh. "I'll take my chances."

"Where is everybody else?" With his luck, they'd move the party out here.

"Off to their rooms. The party pretty much broke up after you left."

Guilt swept over him. Some host he was. "I'm sorry I was such a jerk." Staring at his hands, he flexed his fingers. "I don't know what's wrong with me."

"Same thing that's wrong with me, I expect." She leaned close. "I was dying to touch you and couldn't."

His gaze jumped to hers. "You were?"

She smiled and leaned closer, her breasts brushing his chest, her gaze sliding to his lips. "Yes."

His heart lurched.

"Know what else I think?"

"What?"

"I agree. Let's do it."

7

LET'S DO IT, *let's do it.*

Tony swallowed—somehow managing to do so without choking on his tongue. "When?" he managed.

"Let's not set a time. We'll just let it happen naturally."

"Okay." He stared at her—her flushed skin and smoky eyes. "How about now?"

"Well—"

He grabbed her hand and jumped to his feet. "Now's good for me," he said, pulling her along beside him. "Is now good for you?"

"Well, I guess. Slow down, would you?"

He strode through the back door and into the lobby. "I'm not sure I can."

As they waited for the elevator, he held her hand and kept her close by his side. He ordered his heart to stop racing and his body to relax.

Neither listened.

Lose his finesse, hell, he was going to lose his mind.

His erection throbbed nearly to the point of pain. *Let's do it, let's do it.*

He was finally going to have her. One night only. No holds barred.

It occurred to him that since it was one-thirty in the

morning, he was technically getting cheated out of his full night, but he'd renegotiate that later.

There is no later, remember? Tomorrow it's back to good buddies and partners.

Right.

Finally, *finally* the elevator arrived with a soft ping. He pulled Francesca inside, pressed the third-floor button and watched the numbers light in succession. *Breathe, man, breathe. Stay in control.*

"Tony—"

He held up his hand to stop her, though he didn't look at her. One glance into those smoky blues and control would go *pfft*. "Hush. I'm chanting."

"You're—" She crossed her arms over her chest. He could envision her look of frustration.

Control. Breathe.

"Your room or mine?" he asked as the doors parted.

"Never mind. Mine's closer."

Not bothering to search for his key, he punched in his code, then flung open the door.

Control. Breathe.

She walked away from him, crossing to the center of the room and stopping just in front of the coffee table. "Should we get undressed, or do you want to just flip my skirt over my head and do it right here on the table?"

"I—" His gaze shot to the table. It was iron and glass and didn't look too comfortable, but then—

"Tony!"

He flinched, then reluctantly met her gaze. Smoky eyes, but she was scowling.

Control. Breathe.

"Relax," she said in a softer tone. She took two un-sure steps in his direction, then laid her hand carefully on his shoulder, as if he were a bomb about to explode, which was pretty much how he felt.

She slid her hand down his arm, gripping his hand and drawing him toward the sofa. "Sit."

He did, his whole body tight with need, and her touch against his skin only increasing the pressure.

She left him on the sofa, kicked off her shoes, then walked around it, sliding her hands along the tops of his shoulders. "You're tight as a drum," she said, flex-ing her hands.

He moaned. "No kidding."

She kneaded the muscles in his shoulders and neck. "Relax. It's just me."

That statement didn't sound exactly right, but her hands felt so good, he didn't argue.

While she kept up the massage with one hand, she slid the other around to his chest and flicked open but-tons on his shirt.

Control. Breathe.

He started to help her, but she pushed aside his hands. "Relax."

Letting his arms fall by his sides, he dropped his head back against the sofa and closed his eyes.

Then sucked in a harsh breath as her fingertips slid across his bare chest.

"I've been wanting to do that all night," she said, sounding as breathless as he felt.

He blinked his eyes open and looked up at her. Her eyes were closed, her face glowing with pleasure.

He could have lain there forever, watching bliss

flicker across her features. She quite simply fascinated him.

And somehow the control he'd sought so desperately washed over him. She was a woman to be enjoyed, savored...treasured.

With her eyes still shut, she rubbed both hands across his shoulders, down his chest, leaning over so she could reach his stomach and sides. Her breasts brushed his head, but he clamped down on the urge to caress her in return. She took such obvious pleasure in touching him, he didn't want to distract her.

Control. Breathe.

Using the heels of her hands, she pressed hard against his muscles, kneading and pressing, somehow soothing as well as exciting. Every brush of her breasts against him was sweet torture. He relished her touch even as he trembled with need and longed for more.

When the edge of her fingernail scraped his nipple, he grabbed her wrist. "Please, *bella*. I'm dying here."

"Please, what?" she whispered in his ear, her breath teasing his senses. "Please stop? Please more?"

"Both."

She laughed softly. "My, my, I do think I've confounded the ultra-smooth Tony Galini."

"Looks like." He reached behind him and, grasping her beneath her arm, yanked her over the sofa and into his lap.

She blinked up at him. "Speaking of smooth."

He let his gaze rove over the luscious bundle now in his arms—her golden skin, the single shoulder bared by her dress, the delicious length of her legs. "I was thinking silky, or maybe slinky." He bent close to her face. "I can't believe you're really here."

Her tongue flicked across her bottom lip. "Me neither."

He lowered his head, covering her mouth with his. She tasted like champagne. She felt like heaven. As he sank deeper into the kiss, a small sigh escaped her lips.

He slid his tongue against hers, drawing her warmth and sweetness into his blood. He skimmed his palm along her side, caressing her provocative curves.

Wanting to keep from losing control again, he forced his movements to remain slow and deliberate, concentrating on absorbing each and every sensation: the spicy scent emanating from her skin, the heated stroking of her hand against his chest, the pressure of her body on his thighs.

This was all part of Francesca—his best friend, a woman he knew as no other. Yet, he hadn't known the erotic taste of her lips and the pressure of her body against his until a few days ago. Before the night was over he'd know a great deal more. His control slipped at the idea of just how deep his explorations would go.

He cupped her jaw and left her mouth to trail kisses down her throat. Her hot breath rushed across his cheek; her breathing quickened. As she angled her body to give him better access, her bottom pressed into his groin.

His hardness swelled and throbbed. His body's needs twined themselves around his senses, squeezing out rational thought, heightening every move, every sigh, every heartbeat.

Then she straddled him.

Okay, so much for control.

Francesca pressed the aching center of her body against Tony's erection. "Ah, much better."

"You're telling me," he answered in a strangled voice.

Bracing her hands on his chest, she smiled, then rolled her hips forward. "I like making you lose your breath," she said, her lips barely an inch from his.

"Glad I could—" his hands flexed against her waist, "—help."

She flicked her tongue across his bottom lip, and his erection pulsed.

She hadn't expected to have so much power over him. How many times over the years had she watched other women dazzle him, always wondering what it would be like to affect him that way, to totally capture his attention?

Relinquishing it wouldn't be easy.

She willed away that negative thought. Instead, she nibbled at his lips. Great lips, she realized. Full and sensitive, intent on pleasure. *Her* pleasure. She wanted those lips to trail down her body. How many sensitive areas could the clever, experienced Tony find?

She shivered delightfully at the thought.

Sinking her tongue past his lips, she wrapped her arms around his neck and pressed her throbbing breasts against his chest. Less clothes, that's what they needed. She wanted her bare chest rubbing his. She wanted her whole naked body rubbing his.

She started to wriggle off his lap. "Okay, it's time to lose some clothes."

With his hands on her hips, he held her in place.

"Hey, we can do that from here." He smiled, reaching for the zipper that ran down the side of her dress.

His gaze locked with hers as he dragged down the zipper, and she held her breath. The bra was sewn into the top. When the dress was gone, she'd be fully exposed.

How would she compare? she wondered as he pushed the strap down her arm.

The dress pooled at her waist, and his gaze drifted across her body. Her skin heated; her nipples puckered. When his gaze came back to hers, his eyes were dark, desire-filled...hungry. "Wow."

Then he wrapped his hand around the back of her neck and pulled her toward him for his kiss.

She parted his shirt, sliding her breasts across his warm, bare chest. Waves of desire crashed through her body, and she closed her eyes, immersed in the sensations: the burning need between her legs, the aching fullness of her breasts. Her heart pounded and her breath came in short bursts.

Sensual hunger grabbed her by the throat, demanding satisfaction. She had to get closer. She needed more of him.

She jerked his shirt off his shoulders, shoving the material down his arms and off his body.

In response, he crushed her against his chest, his lips driving her maddeningly out of control. He drugged her with his desire, compelled her to respond. She was falling deeper under his spell and couldn't even see why she shouldn't.

Gasping, he tore his mouth from hers. "I need you, Ches. Let's go to the bedroom."

"No." She yanked his belt from its loops, then unbuttoned his pants. "Here. Now."

"Now's good," he choked out as she wrapped her hand around the hard, hot length of him.

She slid her hand down, then up, running the edge of her fingernail into the slit at the top of his erection.

He closed his eyes and dropped his head back. "I have to meditate again."

"Condoms?" she asked against his neck.

He shook his head, and her heart thumped in panic. "Can't remember," he gasped.

"We need them."

"Mmm. Yeah."

"We really need them," she said, and, groaning with regret, let go of him.

He bolted upright. "We do?" He shook his head as if to clear his thoughts. "Yes, of course we do."

Glaring, she planted her hands on her hips. "You don't have any in your bedside table?"

"No."

"Wallet?"

"No."

"What about Sandy, Mandy and Candy?"

He frowned. "It was Misty, Camy and Ally, and they invited me to the hot tub, not their bed."

Francesca rolled her eyes. Power outages, lust for a friend, picky critics, imminent arrival of resort guests, unprepared men. She couldn't take much more.

But her palms burned against Tony's skin. Her body pulsed. She couldn't back out now.

She rose and shimmied out of her dress, then darted into the bedroom for a robe.

When she returned, Tony hadn't moved. He stared up at her hopefully. *"Please* do that shimmy thing again. And slowly."

"Deal. But for now we're going to the gift shop."

"You want to *shop*?"

She grasped his hand and tugged him to a stand. "For condoms."

"Oh." Rising, he tidied his clothes, and they hurried across the room.

She pulled open the door, poking her head out. "It's clear."

Behind her, Tony put his hands on her waist. His erection brushed her bottom. "This would be exciting if I wasn't on the edge of exploding."

Francesca swallowed the urge to throw caution to the wind. She was desperate, not stupid. "Same goes."

They darted down the hall and into the elevator without seeing anyone. Surely everyone else was asleep by now. As soon as the elevator began its descent, Tony jumped to the other side of the car.

"What are you doing over there?"

"Chanting."

She bit back a smile; she was just as frustrated.

When the elevator reached the lobby, she poked her head out. Nobody was around. After tomorrow they'd never get away with this mission undetected. Tomorrow the resort would be full of guests and employees twenty-four hours a day. They'd have to stock up.

As she started across the marbled lobby floor—with Tony behind her mumbling rhythmically—she remembered their agreement. One night only. *Right.* But that was all she'd need. One night to get rid of this nagging curiosity about Tony, to finally sate her long-held lust for him, then it was back on the path to The One.

A workable plan. A good plan.

She ignored the annoying portion of her conscience that reminded her of the recent problems with her business plans. She couldn't even keep the power on consistently! How in the world was she going to deal with a post-sex relationship with Tony?

They'd reached the gift shop, so she flung her worries aside as she unlocked the door. She walked past the displays of wine-bottle holders and picnic baskets, then around a carousel of cards to the personal products section. Aspirin, cough medicine, tampons, sunscreen...condoms.

She snagged a box, then spun, only to plow into Tony. "Got 'em."

He looked at the box, then back to the selection. "Large? What about extra large?"

"Oh, good grief," she said as she switched boxes, though she couldn't deny an upgrade in size wasn't exactly a *bad* thing.

"Ribs or no ribs?" he asked her.

"I'm not picky. Let's just go."

"We came all the way down here," he argued, perusing the choices, "we might as well get the right ones."

Angling her head, she looked over the many, many boxes. "Who in the world ordered eight different kinds of condoms?"

"I did."

"Why?"

"This is a romantic resort."

That actually sort of made sense, but she really thought they could do without the glow-in-the-dark and smiley-face-printed varieties.

Finally, he selected a box—extra large, ribbed, clear—and they turned to leave.

And through the glass walls saw Allison and Rob wearing bathrobes and tiptoeing across the lobby in their direction.

Francesca slammed to a halt. "What are they doing down here?"

Tony sighed. "This seduction isn't going *at all* the way I planned."

There was no way they could get out the open door without being seen. Where could they hide? She scanned the small shop, considering the rows of swimsuits and resort clothes hanging on the back wall, but decided on the cashier's counter. They would be well-hidden behind it as long as Allison and Rob didn't decide to check out the selection of beach bags.

"Come on," she said to Tony, tugging him toward the counter.

They ducked down just as Allison and Rob reached the door. "I can't believe we're doing this," Allison said in a whisper. "It's like stealing."

"We'll give Francesca and Tony some money tomorrow," Rob answered. "Do you think they're really going to have them?"

"I hope. How could you have forgotten condoms?"

Open-mouthed, Francesca stared at Tony. Them too? Good grief.

"I'm not used to buying them. You were the one who said you wanted to go off the pill for a while."

"Don't you start."

"We could always start our baby-making plans early," Rob suggested, his voice much lower than before.

A sigh, then a moan.

Francesca leaned her forehead against the shelf behind the counter. *This is not happening.*

"Cut it out," Allison said, though she didn't sound too irritated.

Now Francesca could hear kissing sounds, some heavy breathing, another moan. From behind her, Tony lightly bit her ear, and she closed her eyes.

Okay, she wanted him, she *really* did, but this was just too bizarre.

"Mmm, baby, you taste good," Rob said.

They were going to have to show themselves, Francesca decided, though her brain was a bit fogged with desire and Tony's hot breath on her neck, so she made no move to follow through.

Allison giggled. "Let's keep looking."

"Fine, but then I say we try out that counter over there."

Francesca slapped her hand over her mouth to keep from gasping aloud. In panic, she glanced at Tony, who just shrugged.

"You're crazy," Allison said.

Okay, *no way* was she hiding behind a counter in her bathrobe, crouched next to Tony in his rumpled clothes and carrying a fresh box of condoms while two of her closest friends had sex just above her head.

"Rob, back here," Allison said.

Rob whistled, presumably at the numerous choices

available. "Tony's been shopping I see. Knew I could count on him."

Tony grinned.

Francesca rolled her eyes.

"Oh, look, Rob. Glow-in-the-darks."

"That could be fun."

Francesca shook her head. *I can't possibly be here.*

More kissing and heavy breathing from Allison and Rob.

Francesca drew a deep breath, preparing herself for the moment she'd have to pop out from her hiding place. What would she say? *Fancy meeting you here? Good to see the sparks are still alive after all this time? Anybody care for an orgy?*

No, no, definitely not.

"Come over here, baby."

"Rob, I'm not making love on the counter in the gift shop."

Francesca nearly cheered.

"How about the hot tub?"

Allison giggled, and within seconds they were out the door.

Several moments of silence passed while Francesca fought to get her breathing back under control.

"The counter in the gift shop? I never knew Rob was so adventurous."

Francesca elbowed him in the stomach. "We almost got caught." She flopped onto her back on the carpeted floor. "I can't take much more of this."

"Oh, I bet you can." Tony loomed over her, his eyes intently focused on hers. "And would it really have been so bad—Allison and Rob finding out about us?"

Francesca's heart raced, from his nearness, from the questions in his eyes. "There is no us, remember? One night only. That's what we agreed."

"I know."

"Are you having second thoughts?" Maybe he'd decided she wasn't worth all this.

"Hell no." His head descended, his mouth capturing hers, his tongue sliding past her lips.

As usual, he nearly blew the top of her head off. The blood in her veins soared from simmer to boil. She wrapped her arms around his neck, loving the heavy feel of his body on top of hers.

But she'd also waited a long time for this moment, to have Tony all to herself. And she didn't want that moment consummated on the floor of the gift shop.

"Upstairs," she muttered against his mouth.

He lifted his head and smoothed her hair off her forehead. The look on his face was something resembling tenderness. "Anywhere you want, *bella.*"

They made the journey back upstairs quickly, barely touching, as if they understood, by unspoken agreement, that the next time they met skin-to-skin nothing would stop them.

The moment the door to Tony's room clicked shut, she wrapped her arms around his neck, and he wrapped his around her waist, lifting and carrying her to the bedroom.

He set her on the edge of the bed, and she watched, transfixed, while he tore off his shirt, then flung it aside. With the tanned, tight planes of his chest and stomach revealed, she swallowed. The man had some kind of body.

He left his pants on and stalked toward her, his determined gaze locked with hers. She was used to seeing him amused, confident, charming. This seriousness took her breath away.

Kissing her, he cupped the back of her head, urging her back onto the bed, as he braced his body on his forearms. His mouth was warm, persuasive; his body hot. She laid her palms against his chest, the coarse hairs tickling her skin as his body heated hers.

"I wanted to see that shimmy thing again," he said against her jaw, his breath rushing over her. "But I'm not letting you up now."

"Later," she breathed as he worked loose the tie to her robe, then pulled apart the lapels. His gaze moved over her, and her nipples tightened under his scrutiny.

His gaze flicked back to hers. "Beautiful," he said, cupping one breast, his finger sliding over her nipple.

She arched her back, trying to press herself harder against him, silently pleading for more. He increased the pressure and changed the rhythm, moving his thumb in a circular motion. Her breathing hitched in her throat. Her femininity dampened and throbbed.

As the passion crashed over her, she clutched the bedspread, wondering if she should beg him to slow down or plead with him to speed up. Did she want him to prolong or end the sweet torture? She couldn't grasp a coherent thought. The blood in her body had pooled to just a few intimate, sensitive areas.

She'd assumed he'd be a powerful and skilled lover, but she hadn't expected this wild hunger, so intense he could bring her to the brink of climax by merely touching her breasts.

When his mouth replaced his hand, she couldn't hold back a moan. His teeth scraped across her nipple, then his tongue flicked back and forth, and up and down.

She clutched his shoulder. "Tony."

"*Bella*," he returned, then his tongue glided across her chest to give the same intoxicating attention to her other breast.

Her already sensitized skin caught fire. The coil of desire deep in her belly tightened, seizing her, holding her tightly in its grip.

She slid her fingers into his hair, clenching the silky strands. "Please, Tony. Now."

He lifted his head, smiling down at her. "Now's good."

While he helped her to a sitting position and dragged the bathrobe off her shoulders, she fumbled with his belt. Their hands bumped and arms tangled as they fought with each other's clothing, but within seconds they were both stripped to the skin—except for the condom they'd fought so hard to get.

They sat, side by side, breath heaving, watching each other...for about two and a half seconds.

Then, he was on top of her, his weight pressing her deliciously into the mattress, his erection hot and hard against her stomach. His mouth pressed down on hers, and his tongue forced hers to tangle with his. His hands seemed everywhere at once, cupping her breasts, gliding down her sides, clutching her bottom. His fingers trailed between her legs, rubbing her clitoris once, then twice.

She held her breath and arched up; he slid down. His hardness teased the entrance to her body.

His gaze briefly met hers and he kissed her—one, hard forceful kiss. Then he surged inside.

Her body clamped around him, squeezing him, holding him, as if now that she had him she had no intention of letting him go. She would climax in moments, and she wanted him with her when she exploded. She hooked her legs around his hips, and he slid deeper into her body.

She closed her eyes at the intense stab of pleasure.

He groaned into her ear.

Rocking against her, he moved with controlled deliberation. She was both frustrated and appreciative. His easy pace helped hold off her climax, and she loved the warmth and fullness of his body connected to hers, but she was also greedy. She wanted that kick, the waves of pleasure she knew awaited her.

He whispered Italian endearments in her ear, his breath hot and harsh.

She clutched his waist, her palms damp with both his sweat and hers.

Then his movements sped up. He threw his head back, strain clearly showing on his face. Her hips met with his in time, rising to collide, to excite, to rush toward the end, the pinnacle.

The coil holding all the powerful sensations captive tightened one last time, then released, pulsing wildly. She gasped as the sensations echoed outward.

Tony moaned, his hips driving his erection hard into her as her inner walls gripped him tight. With his arm around her lower back, he held her against him as his own completion burst through him.

At the end, he collapsed on top of her, though he pressed his shoulder into the mattress to take most of his weight. All she felt was his warmth, his heart beating solidly against hers.

8

TONY RUBBED his cheek against Francesca's shoulder. "That'll hold me for the next twenty minutes or so."

Her breath whooshed out. "Twenty minutes?"

He kissed the top of her breast. "Or so."

She giggled, and the delightful sound echoed off the walls, making him smile widely.

He lifted his head, staring down at her. *What a beauty she is.*

Still laughing, she gazed up at him and trailed her fingers through the hair at his temples. The brush of her nails against his scalp sent a tingle rolling down his spine.

A beauty. A friend. Now, a lover.

He waited for panic to intrude on this moment of bliss. He waited for regret to snake its way through his body. But he felt only satisfied. Lucky. Happy.

Shouldn't that scare him? Didn't he need to find a way to keep up the light, easy mood?

The trouble was, he didn't feel light or easy.

He wanted to hold her to him, to ask her for promises and futures. He didn't understand the feelings crowding his chest. They weren't part of Tony-the-charming-playboy's makeup. But he knew they were serious, and he knew he'd have to address them.

But later.

He slid his hand across her flat, warm stomach. "One night means the whole night, right?"

Her gaze searched his for a moment before she responded. "Yes."

He sensed her hesitancy and wasn't about to let her feelings go without comment. They'd always been honest before, and he had no intention of letting that part of their relationship change. "Is that what you want?"

"If you do."

"I do."

"Me, too."

His heart settled back into place. He didn't want her to go.

Brushing her hair back from her face, he kissed her lightly. "Good. But first, we need a snack." He jumped off the bed, then pulled on his pants.

Bleary-eyed, she raised up on her elbows. "Food? You want food?"

He waggled his eyebrows. "For starters."

After slipping on his shirt, he kissed her forehead, then strode from the room. Downstairs, he headed straight for the kitchen, where he searched for champagne, fruit, crackers and cheese. He carried the spread on a silver platter, the champagne in a bucket of ice and the glasses between his fingers.

When he entered the room, he found Francesca wrapped in her robe, sitting on the edge of the bed.

She glanced up as he approached her. Her eyes weren't smoky, but uncertain. "What are we doing?"

He set the food and drinks on the dresser, then sat next to her. He needed to move slowly here, not scare her off, not make too much of anything. Francesca didn't impulsively sleep with men. Actually, she didn't do *anything* impulsively. She was the very definition of cautious and planned.

Not to mention she'd been searching for The One Wednesday night, and he certainly couldn't be him. He had a great bachelor life. Women he wanted wanted him. Settling on just one wasn't in his genes—just ask his father.

So he found his well of charm—deep as it was—and tapped it ruthlessly. He slid his thumb along her jaw. "We're enjoying each other."

"And then?"

He wanted to say something flip and confident, but he settled for the honesty he'd vowed to maintain. "I don't know."

"We'll always be friends, right?"

"Right." He pressed a kiss to her cheek, then retrieved their snack. "I brought fruit. And your favorite champagne." After he popped the cork and poured two glasses, handing her one, he dropped onto the bed beside her. "A toast?"

"To good friends," she said, her gaze on his.

"Intimate friends."

The crystal pealed in the silent room. The tension between them took on a palpable shape, and as they sipped, she looked away from his stare. She still seemed nervous and unsure. Though he felt the same on some level, he wasn't about to let the confusing feelings settling in his belly control him.

"Let me feed you." He selected a strawberry from the tray, dipped it into his champagne, then held it next to her lips. After a moment's pause, she opened her mouth, biting into the fruit. He nearly groaned aloud when her lips brushed his fingers and a burst of sweet nectar filled the air. As the juice flowed over his hand, he licked the syrup from his fingers, keeping his gaze locked with hers. Then, unable to resist, he leaned forward, kissing her, drinking the fruit juice and wine from her lips.

He slid his hand between the opening of her robe, skimming the edge of her breast. "You taste that sweet all over," he whispered against her throat.

Her head dropped back. "I can't think when you touch me."

Pulling her robe off her shoulders, he flicked his tongue across her earlobe. "Then don't."

After grabbing another strawberry, he again dipped the fruit into his glass, but instead of feeding it to her, he slid it along the base of her throat, down the center of her chest, watching a drizzle of reddened champagne glide down her stomach.

Then he urged her back onto the bed and followed the same path with his tongue, licking the sugary juice from her skin.

She shivered. His erection swelled.

Hovering over her, he took a bite of the fruit before feeding her the rest. She chewed slowly, seeming mesmerized by him, or maybe she was just shocked that he'd turned her into his personal banquet table.

Next, he selected a grape, which he rolled around each of her nipples before feeding it to her.

When he drizzled champagne onto her stomach, she gasped. "That's cold."

He bent toward her. "It won't be for long." Then he drank the champagne from her body.

She pressed her hands against his shoulders. Her muscles tightened. Her breathing grew shallow and rapid.

He loved every second of it.

He delighted in the soft, womanly curves of her body. The silkiness of her skin. The scent of her perfume mixed with the fruit.

Giving her pleasure was a heady experience. One he wanted to repeat again and again. He was very afraid that when dawn arrived he wouldn't be sated, he'd be even more desperate to have her, knowing, not just suspecting, the heights they could soar together.

With another champagne-drenched strawberry, he headed toward the most private, sensitive part of her body. He skimmed the fruit along the lips of her femininity.

She arched her back. "Oh, God."

Tony slid the fruit up and down, then paused at the nub where her pleasure pooled. Breathing hard from the effort of keeping his own hunger under control, he worked the fruit over the very tip.

Her body trembled. Her skin flushed deep red. She was on the brink of release.

He intended to push her over.

Tossing the strawberry aside, he replaced the fruit with his tongue. He parted her, exposed her... pleasured her.

In seconds, she was gasping for air. Tremors moved through her body. Then she exploded. She moaned as she reached the peak, and he moved upward so he could watch her face, watch the overwhelming satisfaction wash over her.

She was stunning.

He kissed the last few harsh breaths from her lips and smoothed back her hair. When her eyes flicked open, he saw they were smoky, as he now knew they always were when she was aroused. She blinked and smiled, then trailed her hand lightly down his face.

Then he found himself flat on his back with her straddling him.

"What?" He glanced up at her face.

"More" was all she said before her head descended and her mouth captured his.

Whereas his seduction had been slow, easy and patient, hers was full of restless energy. She tore his shirt open without ever breaking her kiss, then she attacked—there was really no other word for it—his belt buckle. She stripped off his pants and underwear, flinging them to the floor, before slithering out of her robe.

Naked, she climbed back on top of him, her eyes gleaming as she stared down at him. He'd never seen this wild side of her. But he liked it. A lot.

Especially when she rubbed her warm, wet femininity across his erection.

He closed his eyes and clutched her hips, holding her tight against him. Oh, man, he wouldn't be able to last much longer if she kept moving like that.

"I wonder how you taste," she said, leaning forward. Her breasts hung down, brushing the hairs on his stomach as she dragged her tongue across his chest and circled his nipple.

He flexed his hands against her hips as a ripple of pleasure shot down his body. How much more could he take?

She rolled her hips against his erection.

He sucked in a breath. Not a whole hell of a lot.

Fumbling behind him, then beside him, he searched for the box of condoms.

Obviously realizing his mission, she leaned forward briefly, then sat back, the box in her hand. "Impatient?"

Distracted by the brief brush of her breasts against his face, he swallowed. "You could say that," he gasped.

She pushed a condom from the foil packet, then scooted back, gripped the base of his erection and rolled the protection down. The whole process didn't take more than a few seconds, but it seemed like weeks. The touch of her delicate fingers against his sensitive flesh had him gritting his teeth to keep from exploding on the spot.

Before he'd fully recovered from her touch, she braced her hands against his shoulders and plunged down in one smooth stroke. She sat still for a moment, her head thrown back, her eyes closed.

He fought against the need to move. As she began to rock her hips forward and back, he mentally chanted his control mantra, wanting to let her set the pace. Her long, dark hair trailed over her shoulders, brushing her breasts as she moved. Her back was arched, and her fingernails dug into his chest.

All too soon, he sensed her impatience with the

rhythmic movement. Did she want more speed? Deeper penetration?

He gave her both, undulating his hips rapidly, desperate to hold back his climax until he heard her breathing quicken, and a low moan escape from deep in her throat. Only a second later, after she threw her head back and her inner muscles grabbed him tight, squeezing and releasing in quick pulses, did he close his eyes and let his body explode.

FRANCESCA GAVE one last wave to Allison and Rob before closing the limo door. As the long, black car pulled away from the resort, she couldn't hold back a sigh of relief. She felt as if her erotic night with Tony was stamped on her forehead, and she didn't want her friends asking questions she couldn't answer.

She wanted to regret the step she'd taken last night, but she couldn't. The fantasy night was too precious, too satisfying, too brief to ruin with remorse.

By joint agreement between her and Tony, she'd slid out of his bed around seven this morning, and gone to her own room to shower and dress for the day. They'd met in the restaurant at eight for coffee and pastries while waiting for the others to arrive. She'd hoped they'd find their old rhythm, but her hands had been shaking when she'd wrapped them around her mug. She hadn't wanted to eat and had felt even less like talking.

She'd wanted Tony. His touch, his exclusive attention, his assurances that she could finally set aside her crush.

In front of their friends, she'd forced out a performance of normalcy. During the morning's cooking class and wine tasting, she'd smiled and nodded, while the knots in her stomach had twined tighter and tighter.

He, on the other hand, had seemed perfectly at ease. He'd laughed and chatted and was his usual flawless, charming self. Was he really able to dismiss her so easily? Was she that forgettable?

But then, it was what they'd agreed upon: one night only, then back to their old relationship.

She was supposed to be on a quest for The One. She wanted to be ready for the moment he appeared in her life, looked at her as though she was the only woman on the planet, and they fell instantly, forever in love.

So what was the deal with those dreamy, little-girl fantasies and fluttery feelings for Tony?

Thank God for work and its intrusions. Pierre von Shalburg was due at two, along with dozens of other guests. She had a million loose ends to tie up.

She headed to the kitchen first, knowing Tony had gone to see Joe at the winery. She needed to stay busy, keep her mind on her professional goal—making a success of Bella Luna. Her personal life and feelings would just have to wait.

Chef Carlos and Kerry were working side-by-side in the kitchen, with Kerry chopping vegetables and the chef making pasta. At least there was some harmony in her world.

"How did we do?" Kerry asked as she approached.

Francesca smiled at him. "Wonderfully. They raved over your dishes, Chef Carlos. You and Kerry make an excellent team."

Not a morning person—actually his mood wasn't much better *any* time of the day—Chef Carlos merely grunted.

With her stomach in knots over both Tony and the opening, Francesca didn't need conversation anyway. She washed her hands, then helped Kerry with the vegetable chopping.

Minutes later, the phone's intercom buzzed. "Ms. D'Arcy?"

"Yes," Francesca called out.

"Mr. Duncan from Chateau Fontaine is returning your call on line two," the operator said.

"Thanks." Since she still hadn't heard from the power company, she'd called Finnegan Duncan to find out if he'd had any electrical problems recently. She wiped her hand on a towel, then grabbed the phone receiver from the wall phone. "Fin, thanks for calling me back."

"I guess you lost power last night, too," he said in his deep, steady voice.

"For three hours. You?"

"Same time. My contact at the power company says it was a scheduled outage to repair storm-damaged lines, though I never got any notice."

Francesca blinked. "You've actually talked to a *person* at the power company?"

He laughed, and Francesca could envision his bright green eyes—the only light feature in an otherwise dark, almost severe face—twinkling.

Come to think of it, there was something very appealing about the large, quiet Irishman. She remembered blushing the first time they'd met, when he'd examined her with that unusual green gaze from head to toe more carefully than most doctors looked at their patients.

Could he be The One? Could he be her cure for finally getting over Tony?

With a sigh, she shook her head, remembering the feel of Tony's tongue as he licked strawberry juice and champagne off her breasts. Fat chance of forgetting *that*.

"Any more scheduled outages I should know about?" she asked Fin, desperate to get her mind back on the subject at hand—namely, her all-important career.

"Your guess is as good as mine. You ready to open?"

"Provided we keep the power on."

"You'll be fine. Just make sure your back-up generator checks out and offer free drinks whenever anything goes wrong."

"Spoken like a true Irishman," she said, but the knot in her stomach loosened.

"It works."

"I'm sure. Thanks." She paused. They were competitors, but friendly competitors. "You'll let me know if you hear anything else?"

"Of course."

"Come down for a drink sometime this weekend if you can. We need all the support we can get."

"I'll try."

After they said their goodbyes, Francesca smiled as she hung up the phone. Fin was right. She would be fine.

He'd run the Chateau for the last five years, and she

knew she could learn a great deal from his calm out-look. Her problem was she wanted everything under her control. Like electricity. Like guests' reactions. Like critics' opinions.

Like Tony's feelings.

She'd thought she could control the direction of her love life by finding The One, too, and look where that had gotten her. Deeper in lust with her best friend, even knowing no future was possible.

Next week he'd be romancing another blonde, bru-nette or redhead. She'd be forgotten—except as good ole Ches, best friend and personal cheerleader.

Time to let any lingering dreams go.

Time to let him go.

HE COULDN'T let her go.

Tony had forced himself to be productive all morn-ing—double-checking the winery tour schedule with Joe, supervising the grounds crew while they did some last-minute trimming and pool cleaning, going over the final reservations list. He'd even personally deliv-ered welcoming baskets to each reserved room and suite, as a thank-you to their very first guests. Any minute, he expected people to begin arriving, their eyes alight with expectation over their stay. The resort was nearly fully booked—with only two rooms on the second floor still available—and the staff was ready to go. But he was miserable.

One night only.

Whose dumb idea had that been?

His, of course.

In pondering the complete failure of his plan, and

where, exactly, he'd gone wrong, he realized he never pondered. Or worried. He just sort of...did things. Did he really have to develop a conscience along with his newfound sense of responsibility? And all in the same month?

Sinking into a chair on the porch just outside the lobby, he pondered anyway. Today he was supposed to go back to his free-wheeling lifestyle. He was supposed to set aside all that he'd shared with Francesca last night—the quiet whispers, the silky feel of her skin gliding against his, the warmth of her touch, the champagne and strawberries.

He'd set aside one-night stands before—not as often as people probably thought, but still, he had. Why couldn't he forget this one?

You know her, he reminded himself.

So? He'd known other women before and after he'd slept with them, too. Why was she so different? Why couldn't he forget this one?

He rose and wandered across the pool deck and into the herb garden. The sweet scent of basil and the sharp scent of rosemary rose in the air. She spent a lot of time here. She'd let the landscaping team till the earth, but she'd sown the seeds personally. He'd seen her pruning the plants and selecting bunches of ripening leaves to use in recipes.

Should he just tell her he was having second thoughts about their one-night-only agreement?

No, that wouldn't do him any good.

She didn't enter into affairs with men like him. She took her life, her career, everything seriously. She was looking for The One, and he couldn't promise her anything. He didn't want to.

He had to let her go.

"Mr. Galini?"

Miserable with his decision, Tony glanced up to see Derrick, one of the young bellhops standing next to him. "Hmm?"

"The first guest is here."

FRANCESCA STRAIGHTENED the sleeves of her navy blazer and walked out the French doors toward the pool. She hadn't seen Tony since the first guests had begun to arrive, and she wanted to double-check the dinner-reservation list.

Ha! That's a lie! You just want to see him.

Sure she did. Pierre von Shalburg still hadn't arrived, and her nerves were so on edge they were practically slicing her skin. She wanted a pep talk from her partner.

Of course, business hadn't been on her mind earlier as she'd wandered over to the winery and walked amongst the fermenting tanks and aging barrels, as if she had nothing better to do. She'd been surprised when she hadn't found Tony. He loved it there, inhaling the sharp flavor of the grapes, tasting the contents of a barrel to determine its readiness.

She wanted to inhale *him*, taste *him*.

Fat chance. One night only. You agreed.

"It's better this way," she said to herself. *You want The One. You deserve The One. You don't want anything to do with The Temporarily-Hot-and-Terrific One.*

She approached the pool deck, craning her neck

looking for Tony. She saw a couple sitting on the edge of the pool, a bronzed woman floating on a raft, and a laughing group of bikini-clad women in lounge chairs.

Where was he? The guys at the front desk said he'd come out here. Not long ago, she might have wondered if he was goofing off somewhere, but she couldn't deny his commitment to the resort over the last few weeks.

Then, as she took a few steps closer to the pool, she noticed a black-topped head in the center of the giggling loungers.

Her heart gave her a good, swift kick in the ribs.

It was good to know he'd had as much trouble forgetting about last night as she had. *Ha!*

Feeling ridiculous, but not about to admit how much she wanted to avoid him, she walked purposefully in his direction.

After a brisk count of highlighted heads she realized he was surrounded by five women. All of them with busty, tight bodies and perfect hair, accessorized by expensive jewelry and varying shades of shiny Lycra. The prince and his harem.

*And you thought he was attracted to your turtleneck.
Ha!*

When she reached the group, the blonde closest to Tony laid her hand on his arm. "Are you going to give us a personal tasting later?"

Francesca raised her eyebrows. "Tony," she began, crossing her arms over her chest, "do you think I could drag you away from your work for a moment?"

His gaze—which might even have been remorseful—met hers. "Of course." He bathed his pouting harem in a charming smile. "I'll be right back, ladies."

The blonde who wanted a tasting glared at Francesca with open hostility.

Francesca ignored her and walked a few feet away with Tony.

"Problem?" he asked, angling his head.

He didn't smile or tease her, and she certainly had no intention of teasing him. Beneath her irritation, she was hurt—a condition she didn't want to admit to him or herself.

Had they really woken up in the same bed only that morning? Their intimacy seemed like a lifetime ago.

"No problem," she forced herself to say lightly. "I just wondered how heavy the dinner reservations were."

His gaze swept her face briefly. "The maître d' has the list."

"I wanted to hear about it from you. What are people saying? Are they impressed? Excited?"

"Our clientele tends to be on the jaded side, remember? But, yes, I think they're impressed. Everyone I've talked to is eating in the restaurant tonight, and they're interested in hearing the band later."

Francesca let a bit of her tension escape. Tony read people well. He'd know if the guests thought the resort wasn't up to their standards.

"No sign of von Shalburg?" He glanced at his watch. "He was due at two."

Francesca bit her lip. "He's only twenty minutes late."

"And he seemed like such a prompt guy," Tony said dryly.

"You don't think he's changed his mind?"

Tony's eyes softened, and he laid his hands on her shoulders. "No, I don't. Stop worrying. Everything is beautiful. Perfect."

Francesca glanced up at him, trying to pretend she didn't feel his body heat seeping into hers. He was so close. But unreachable.

"You look tired," he said softly. "Are you okay?"

She nodded. They hadn't slept very much last night, and she doubted very much if she'd sleep tonight either. She'd know he was next door. Too close. Too tempting.

Not that he'd be tempted by her. He had the five bikini-clad babes hanging all over him.

Dammit, *she* wanted a harem. Did they have male harems? If so, she was putting in an order right away.

"I should get back to the lobby and wait for von Shalburg." She backed out of his reach. "And you can get back to your work."

He glanced over to the harem, and she could have sworn he winced. But when his gaze came back to hers, his eyes were sparkling. "Guest relations is such a tough job…"

She forcibly ignored the jealousy sneaking its way into her veins. He wasn't hers to feel possessive about. She'd expected this. She'd made a deal, and she was holding up her end of the agreement.

Even if it tore her apart.

"I'll see you later," she said.

"Let me know when von Shalburg arrives."

She turned away. "Sure."

When she reached the back porch, Tony suddenly appeared beside her. "I never did ask you last night— why after all this time?"

Startled by his abrupt appearance and question, Francesca swallowed. She doubted "why not" would work for her. She hadn't let him get away with a flip answer when she'd asked him the same question last night.

But what could she say? She hadn't just suddenly realized her attraction to him after he'd crawled naked into her bed two weeks ago. Why in the world had she ever asked that stupid question anyway?

"You asked me the same thing, remember?" he went on. "Was it the night I accidentally came into your room? Is that what made you look at me differently?"

She stared at his chest. "Uh, no, my attraction had been building for a bit longer."

"How much longer?"

"Mmm. I don't think I could pinpoint the precise moment."

He slid his finger beneath her chin and tipped up her face to his. "When we started working on the resort?"

Yes, yes. That makes sense. That's not humiliating.

But she couldn't seem to force the lie past her lips. He'd been honest with her, after all. "It may have been a little earlier than that."

"How much earlier?" he asked.

"Oh, uh…about ten years."

9

TONY'S MOUTH dropped open, and Francesca winced. "Ten—" He shook his head. "We were only nineteen."

"Okay, maybe eleven."

"Eleven."

She shrugged, feeling her face heat. "About that."

"Eleven," he repeated, running his hand through his hair.

Well, he didn't have to look so damn upset by the idea. Was it really that awful to think—

Then he smiled. Widely. Proudly. "All that time you...wanted me?"

Francesca sighed in disgust. "I must have lost my mind, pumping that ego of yours with even more fuel."

He rocked back on his heels. "So you've been pining for me for eleven years."

"I have *not* been pining."

"What would you call it?"

"Candidacy for serious psychotherapy."

"I think I'm insulted."

"Look, Tony—" She smiled as a group of guests streamed out the lobby doors, then she pulled him into the porch's corner. They were practically in the shrubbery, but she didn't want anyone to hear them. "Don't make a big deal out of this. This attraction thing has been going on a few years, but it wasn't anything compelling enough to act on."

"Until last night."

"I'd always been sort of...curious about how we'd be together, so I figured, what the hell."

"What the hell," he repeated, not looking nearly as thrilled as before. And thank God, too, since Tony was a champion gloater.

"Right. And now I've satisfied my curiosity, so that's that."

Damn, that sounded so sensible. Maybe if she said the words often enough she could believe them and live by them.

"That's that," he said.

"Absolutely."

He said nothing for a moment or two, during which time Francesca silently hoped he'd drop the subject. She'd been honest, but she didn't really want to dwell on it. As close as they were, they had different goals in life. She wanted stability, a successful career, a marriage like her parents had. Tony wanted...well, she wasn't exactly sure what Tony wanted—she wasn't even sure *he* knew what he wanted—but she'd bet freedom was somewhere in the top two.

But her heart began to race as she looked up at him. A smile broke out across his face. "I don't think so, Ches. You never do anything just for the hell of it."

"I just did," she insisted.

"I think there's more to it."

Oooh, that man! Having him know about her longstanding crush was bad enough, but to have him think she was "pining" after him, while he romanced every woman between twenty-five and sixty at the resort was something else entirely.

"Ches, if you're not going to be honest—"

"I was honest."

"After eleven years."

She took an angry step forward. "Maybe I should have made my feelings known sooner." She cocked her head. "Maybe right after you consoled Buffy Anders on her broken engagement. Or between Tawny Clayton's divorce and the lovely Lana Leighton's move into the apartment across from yours. I'd have needed a freaking appointment to put my application in."

He leaned close. His spicy scent washed over her. "Jealous?"

"Hell no."

He drew his fingertip across her jaw. "But you're aroused."

Mortified, she closed her eyes.

"Oh, no, you don't. No shutting me out." He paused, flicking his thumb across her lips. "Back to my point."

She forced her eyes open, then narrowed them. More cracks about her crush?

"As I started to say earlier, I'm ready to be completely honest."

"Oh, yeah?"

"I want another night with you." As her heart rate jumped, he added, "Several more actually."

"You do?" she managed to choke out, just barely holding back *Why?*

"Oh, yeah," he said, so close to her ear he stirred the hair at her nape.

Giving in to this lust was the surest path to heart-ache, but her body could care less about what was wise. It wanted what it had last night.

Her breathing quickened. Her breasts throbbed. Her femininity ached.

Then her mind traitorously jumped in to help. It sup-plied visions of her and Tony naked, damp and sticky with champagne. Tony's muscles tight as he fought to keep control and rhythm, drawing out the pleasure for them both. Tony throwing back his head as he found release.

"You're pondering," he said quietly. "I did a lot of that myself today."

"*You?* What about?"

He slid his hand down her side, shooting tingles through her body. "You. Us."

"Did it help—to ponder, I mean?"

"Not a bit. I tried to talk myself out of wanting you."

She met his gaze and was surprised to see not only desire, but also some apprehension. "Me, too."

"And?"

She'd regret this decision later. *Decision?* Try hor-mone-induced impulse. She was on a mission to find The One. She'd vowed to give up pointless relation-ships that led nowhere beyond physical pleasure and mildly interesting conversation. And with anyone but Tony, she could have stuck to that vow. But Tony was, well...Tony. And, therefore, irresistible. "I'm not hav-ing much luck either."

He smiled, the same smile she'd seen him use on dozens of women over the years. Was that what she was now? Just part of his harem? "So, same time, same place tonight?"

"No." She hesitated just a second before adding, "Same place, but earlier."

"How about now?"

"I was thinking ten or eleven."

"Ten."

"Ms. D'Arcy?"

Turning, Francesca found the bellhop, Derrick, standing behind her. His face was anxious. "He's here."

Still under the influence of Tony, it took her a moment to realize who *he* was. "Mr. von Shalburg?"

"Yes, ma'am."

She could all but see her career conscience shake its head in disgust. *Excuse me? You* forgot *about the most important critic on the eastern seaboard? Are you picking a night in the sack over your professional goals?*

It'll be a *really* great night in the sack, she argued back.

What about making the resort a success?

Oh, shut up.

"Excuse me, ma'am?" Derrick asked, his voice rising to a squeak.

Realizing she'd spoken aloud, her face heated. "Sorry, Derrick, I've got a lot on my mind. Thank you. I'm coming." As Derrick went back into the lobby, she glanced over her shoulder at Tony. "We'll talk...I mean I guess I'll see you later."

He linked arms with her, discreetly pressing a light kiss to her temple. "You absolutely will, but I'm not go-

ing anywhere now. This is our place. We face him together."

A warm glow filled her. Again, she realized her reservations about Tony's level of commitment had
faded. He hadn't lost interest. He hadn't backed away.
Their partnership had flourished and produced Bella
Luna.

She smiled up at him as they walked through the
lobby doors. No matter what else happened from this
moment on they had that much.

And no matter what Pierre von Shalburg said, she
was proud.

"MR. GALINI, could you have more towels brought to
my room? I like white, not beige."

"Right away, Mr. von Shalburg," Tony said, rolling
his eyes as he spoke into his cell phone. He looked
longingly at his untouched martini, sitting on the bar in
front of him. He'd come to the restaurant while waiting
for Francesca to change clothes, but he should have
known he wouldn't even begin to relax before dear ole
von Shalburg interrupted. "Anything else?"

"That will do for now."

"I'm so glad." Tony signed off, then immediately dialed housekeeping. "Mabel," he began when the manager answered, "could you get some white towels to
Mr. von Shalburg's room, please?"

There was a long pause. "They're all white, Mr. Galini."

"I know. Do we have any that are *extra* white? Mr.
von Shalburg says his look beige."

"I'll look for an extra-white set right away, Mr. Galini."

"Thank you so much, Mabel."

Tony ended the call, then quickly sipped his drink. No telling when that damn phone would ring again.

He'd agreed to carry a cell phone all weekend, so von Shalburg could call him anytime he needed something. God help him. Francesca said they needed a great review, and he was determined to do his part to make that happen—even if he hated cell phones and was very sure the critic's constant demands would put a major damper on his evening of seduction with Francesca.

He smiled as he thought of her and their new "arrangement." He'd planned to let her go. Really.

He'd planned to go right back to his bathing beauties, to force himself to forget all about Francesca. She wanted a commitment, and he wanted...well, he liked variety.

But then that eleven-year attraction business had come out, and he knew he was a goner. To think he could have had the naked and flushed Francesca experience years ago made him downright regretful. And anxious to make up for lost time. He'd never been much on self-sacrifice and staying away from her would have amounted to torture.

Though this cell-phone carrying came damn close.

As if it knew he'd thought about it, the annoying thing rang. He pressed the talk button quickly, since some smart guy had set the thing to play "Brick House" instead of ringing like a normal phone. He'd have to get somebody to change that ASAP.

It was von Shalburg on the phone. Surprise, surprise.

"Mr. Galini," he began in an exasperated tone, "I'm afraid these towels won't do either."

"No kidding."

"No, I'm afraid I'm not," he said, Tony's sarcasm apparently lost on him. "These simply aren't fluffy enough."

"But they're white."

"Oh, yes. Perfectly white."

"But not fluffy."

"Definitely not."

Francesca walked up, and Tony temporarily let his eyeballs fall out of his head and ogle her shamelessly. She wore a peacock-blue spaghetti-strap dress made of a flowing, filmy material that clung to her body, yet was still feminine and elegant.

He decided it would look exceptionally good pooled on the floor of his bedroom.

"Mr. Galini, what are we going to do about this towel situation?" von Shalburg said impatiently in his ear.

"I'm sure we can do something." Tony stood and pulled out the barstool next to him for Francesca. "I'll get fluffy ones up to your room right away."

"I should think so."

Tony signed off and brushed a kiss across Francesca's cheek. She smelled as fantastic as she looked. "How long till ten o'clock?" he asked, closing his eyes as a wave of desire rocked his body.

"Three hours and twenty-three minutes."

He opened his eyes and studied hers. Smoky blue longing stared back at him. *Oh, man.*

"Was that Mr. von Shalburg on the phone?"

He inhaled more of the luscious, fruity scent emanating from her skin. He could stand like this for the next ten hours or so. Just stand next to her, absorbing the sight, sound and smell of her. Though before long, he supposed he'd have to get around to tasting and touching, too. "Hmm?"

"Mr. von Shalburg?"

"Oh, him. Yeah." Reluctantly, Tony returned to his seat. Ten o'clock couldn't come soon enough. He ordered two more drinks, then he dialed housekeeping again. "Mabel, I need more towels."

Mabel, bless her, simply sighed. "Mr. von Shalburg?"

"You know it. He wants fluffy towels."

"*Extra*-fluffy?" she returned dryly.

"That would be nice. Can you just throw them in the dryer to puff them up a bit?"

"I'm on top of it."

"You're a gem, Mabel."

"I know," she said and hung up.

Tony flipped the phone closed, then set it on the bar next to his martini. If he dunked it in the martini, would all the circuits fail? He smiled at the thought.

"You don't have to carry that thing around, you know," Francesca said. "He could call the front desk when he needs something."

"No, as you pointed out the other day, I'm in charge of guest relations. He's a guest. I'm going to relate to him." He paused. "Even if it kills me."

"But—"

"Forget him." He brushed her hair off her shoulders. "You look fantastic."

"Thanks." She sipped her drink. "I'm so glad my nervous breakdown isn't showing from the outside."

"You're not having a breakdown." He picked up the phone and waved it in front of her. "I've got von Shalburg handled."

"Not just him. My whole life is careening off course."

He suddenly realized she wasn't talking about the resort. "Because of me."

She played with the stem of her glass. "We're very different, Tony. We have different outlooks and goals."

"I don't have goals."

"See what I mean?"

"I'm kidding." He stroked her back. "I have a goal— the same one as you, I bet. Make Bella Luna a success."

"And when you succeed? What then? If Pierre von Shalburg gives us a good review, Bella Luna could be set."

"I don't know. Martinique sounds good."

"Be serious."

"Why?"

She looked away. He could tell she was frustrated with him. She'd say nothing, but his lack of ambition and direction bothered her. He'd been raised that way—though he'd long ago stopped looking to his parents as models upon which he could pattern his life.

He really didn't see how his goals—or lack thereof— affected their relationship. They were going to have fun, enjoy each other's company and bodies. He didn't need ambition. He had money, friends and access to good wine.

Admittedly, he'd enjoyed the satisfaction of seeing Bella Luna grow into a beautiful resort. And he'd even enjoyed falling into bed at night knowing he'd accomplished something more than getting to his tennis match on time, but did he really want to *work* the rest of his life?

He'd gotten into this business venture mainly to impress his uncle, to experience a bit of the respect Joe commanded. Francesca was right, if Bella Luna was declared a success after this weekend, and he'd proved to his family and friends he could succeed in business, what would he do then? Go back to his old life?

Frowning, he realized he wasn't sure that was what he wanted anymore either. In the back of his mind, he'd always pictured his life going on as before, but he'd changed a lot over the last few months. He looked at his life, his ability to succeed, with new eyes. Once he'd proved he deserved Joe's confidence in him, and had earned everyone's respect, he was almost sure he'd want to keep it.

But could he? Commitment had never been his strong suit.

Aside from the resort, he also knew Francesca wouldn't continue to see a man like the one he'd been for most of his life. That might have even been the reason she'd never admitted her attraction to him. She wanted a man she could respect, both personally and professionally.

He didn't have time to wonder about whether he

could be—or wanted to try to be—that man, since the phone rang again.

Shooting Francesca a look of regret, he answered. "Mr. von Shalburg, how are the towels?"

"Very good. Thank you. But I do so enjoy a quiet before-dinner drink in my room, and unfortunately, I don't see my favorite brand of Scotch behind the bar."

Each suite was equipped, not with a mini bar, but a full-sized bar, containing all the appropriate glasses, accoutrements and mixers. If you wanted onions or olives for your martini, they were there. If you wanted branch water with your bourbon, it was readily available. And he distinctly remembered three different brands of Scotch sitting behind each bar—Johnny Walker, Chivas, and Glenlivet.

"Which brand do you prefer?" Tony asked him.

"Dewar's."

The one he hadn't ordered. Great.

Tony scanned the mirrored wall behind the bartender. No Dewar's. "I'll call you back, Mr. von Shalburg, I'm checking on the availability of that."

"Do we have Dewar's?" he asked Francesca when he clicked off.

"There may be a bottle in the back."

After a search of the storeroom behind the bar, Tony found a bottle. He called Derrick to take the Scotch to von Shalburg's room, then he sank onto his stool. He wouldn't consider himself a hothead by any stretch, but, by damn, if von Nit-Picky called one more time, he wasn't sure he could control a violent response. Every guest couldn't possibly be this aggravating. In fact, the other weekend guests had been gracious and pleased with their accommodations.

He rubbed his temples. *There's one in every crowd.*

Francesca slid her hand over his and squeezed. "Let's give some attention to our other guests."

Smiling, Tony rose and helped Francesca off her bar-stool. "That's the best idea I've heard all night." Then, he leaned close to whisper in her ear. "Except for my idea to lick my way down your body."

She glanced up at him. Her tongue flicked across her lips. "We'll get to that later."

Tony's erection swelled, but somehow he managed to force his mind back on his role as resort host and walk her toward the tables full of diners. *That* was progress. In fact, if that wasn't a complete success in the playboy-turned-businessman saga, he didn't know what was.

He asked the guests about their dinner, he suggested bottles of wine, he talked about the tastings, the tours and the cooking demonstrations. This was what resort ownership was supposed to be. And as he watched Francesca's animated face as she talked with their guests, he realized how lucky he was to share this experience with her. How lucky he was to have her as a business partner, friend and lover.

Of course, all too soon, his luck ran out.

"Pierre von Shalburg. I believe I have a reservation."

At the sound of the familiar voice, Tony turned his head. Von Shalburg was at the maître d's stand. His thinning salt and pepper hair was slicked back from his forehead. His round, wire-framed glasses were perched on the end of his nose, down which he was looking as he glanced around the restaurant. Dressed in a three-piece, blue pinstriped suit—a red bowtie completing the ensemble—he looked like ninety percent of the college professors Tony had ever met, those who took great delight in making everyone around them feel stupid.

Tony smiled wanly as von Shalburg and the maître d' walked through the restaurant, heading toward the critic's reserved table. "I'd better check on him," he said to Francesca.

Her gaze darted in von Shalburg's direction. "Don't crowd him."

"I'm not going to crowd him. I'm going to *greet* him. I can handle that, don't you think?"

"Of course you can. Man, you're sensitive."

Tony clenched his fists. "I'm on the edge of committing a violent crime."

"Just don't go over the edge until after he writes that glowing review."

"And then?"

"Be my guest."

Tony watched von Shalburg settle into his booth and accept his menu from the maître d'. "Do you think I actually have any Soprano-type relatives?"

"That's a bit of a cliché, don't you think?"

"Not if it's true, and I'm really hoping it is."

"Maybe I should greet him."

Tony rolled his shoulders back. "No, I've got it. I'm going in." He stalked toward the critic, using his Francesca chant—*Control. Breathe*—for support. The mantra pounded into his brain with each step.

When he reached the table, he cleared his throat. "Mr. von Shalburg, how's your table?"

The man stared at Tony over the tops of his glasses. "Adequate."

Control. Breathe. "And did you receive your Dewar's?"

"With decent promptness." He paused, pursing his thin lips. "You might tell that young bellhop to try not to tremble so much. It's distracting."

"He's young and nervous, sir." And extremely eager to please. Tony had no intention of criticizing the teenager.

Von Shalburg sighed impatiently. "I suppose so."

The waiter and sommelier both appeared, so Tony slipped away with a muttered "If you need anything...."

He'd gone only a few steps when someone grabbed his arm and yanked him behind a display of wine bottles.

Francesca stared up at him. "Well?" she asked in a low voice.

"What are you doing back here?" he whispered back.

"Watching."

"Spying."

"How else am I going to find out what he thinks? What he's doing?"

He steered her to the back of the restaurant. "We'll get reports from the staff. Let's go into the kitchen. I'm not going to lurk in my own restaurant."

In the kitchen, they stayed clear of Chef Carlos, Kerry and their assistants and stood by the back door.

"He's pissed, isn't he?" Francesca asked, her face resigned, but her eyes bleak.

"He's a fussbudget."

"He's— What?" The beginnings of a smile appeared on her face.

"Sounds like something Joe would say, I guess." He narrowed his eyes as he thought about von Shalburg's criticism of Derrick. "How about—he's a jerk? And I think he enjoys the hell out of bothering us."

"He's an influential critic. It's his job to be picky and thorough."

"Doesn't mean he has to get a kick out of making everybody else's life miserable."

"We need this review, Tony."

He laid his hands on her shoulders. What he really wanted was to pull her into his arms and run with her to his room, but this was the only way he could touch her without making a scene in front of their entire kitchen staff. "You want to hear my theory?"

"Sure."

"I think he's playing us."

Francesca angled her head. "Playing us how?"

"I think part of his review process is to run the reviewee around in circles meeting his every whim and demand."

"Why would he do that?"

Tony shrugged. "He gets off on it, I guess."

"Hmm. I guess that's possible. You've always been able to read people well."

Everybody but her. He really had no idea of her emotions about tonight. He knew she wanted him physically, but how did she *feel* about him? Was she just going along with his desire to continue their intimate relationship? How much did her long-standing attraction to him actually play into all this?

He had no right to ask those questions. The fact that he was even considering them was totally foreign to him. In the past, he'd only considered a woman's feelings on the most basic level. He never really worried about how much she did or didn't care about him, since he always went into relationships with both parties knowing their time together would be fun but temporary.

Now, though, that whole idea seemed shallow, unfulfilling. Is that what he really wanted from Francesca?

"Mr. Galini, Ms. D'Arcy." Von Shalburg's waiter, Mark, walked up to them. "We've got a small problem."

Tony resisted the urge to grab Francesca and run out the back door. "What?"

"Mr. von Shalburg wants to change one of Chef Carlos's dinner specials."

Francesca closed her eyes. "The man has finally gone too far."

Tony's gaze darted between the hesitant waiter and the horrified Francesca. "What's the big deal? Who cares if the guy wants fried chicken livers and pickled beets? Actually, I'm not surprised—"

"*Change* one of artiste Carlos's recipes?" Francesca raised her eyebrows. "*You* want to ask him?"

Tony supposed their primadonna chef wouldn't like von Shalburg messing with his masterpieces, but wasn't there some slogan in the restaurant business about the customer always being right? "I'll do it," he said. Hell, he'd already volunteered to carry a direct link to the critic in his coat pocket. Chef Carlos couldn't be any worse. "What does he want?" he asked Mark.

"A garlic cream sauce for his salmon pasta rather than a wine and shallot sauce," the waiter said, casting a wary glance in Chef Carlos's direction. He was shouting at his staff in Spanish as he waved a long, sharp knife.

"Is that all?" Tony started toward Chef Carlos, noting that Mark and Francesca continued to hover by the door. "Chef Carlos, I need a word, please."

The chef scowled, still holding the knife aloft. "I'm creating."

"Yes, I can see that, but I have a special request from a customer."

Carlos narrowed his eyes suspiciously.

Tony searched his brain for the right words to boost the chef's ego while still getting him to make the change in the dish. Diplomacy and critic butt kissing all in one night. Geez.

Finally, an idea jumped out at him.

He leaned conspiratorially toward Carlos. "We have this crazy critic here, you know, and he actually thinks he knows a better way to prepare *your* salmon pasta." He shook his head, as if he couldn't believe the idiocy of some people. "He wants a garlic cream sauce instead. Can you believe that?"

Chef Carlos' face went from red to purple.

Before the chef could explode, Tony rushed on. "So I was thinking you'd show him a thing or two about up-market cuisine. We'll prepare the dish both ways, then won't he look stupid when your way is, of course, far superior. The pompous jerk probably thinks he's throwing you off, but you'll show him." He guided the chef to the stove and got out a sauté pan. "I can't wait to see the look on his face."

Then, figuring he'd pressed his luck enough, he wandered back to Francesca and Mark.

"He's actually doing it?" Francesca asked, her eyes wide.

"Of course." Tony started to smile but froze when Chef Carlos called his name.

"I'm going with you when the dish is delivered to the table," the scowling chef said.

"Well..." Tony scrambled for a reason to keep the temperamental chef in the kitchen—away from any critic or patron he might become overenthusiastic with. He glanced at the knife still clutched in Carlos's hand. Or carve up like a turkey.

Carlos turned, walking back to the stove before Tony could come up with an excuse.

Beside him, Mark looked worried. "Uh, Mr. Galini, do you think we should let those two meet?"

"I'll disarm Chef Carlos before we come out."

Mark started off. "Okay. Maybe if we keep Mr. von Shalburg's mouth full, too."

"Not a bad idea."

Once Mark had gone, Francesca turned to Tony and smiled, then she leaned forward, brushing his mouth with hers. "You're really amazing, Tony Galini."

The emotion on her face was an unfamiliar one, but still Tony recognized it.

Francesca was proud of him.

And he suddenly realized he could survive a hundred Pierre von Shalburgs, as long as she was by his side.

10

FRANCESCA STOOD on the balcony of Tony's room, watching a puff of clouds blow across the darkened vineyards. She sipped from her wineglass, letting the aroma and buttery smoothness of her favorite chardonnay slide down her throat.

She'd left Tony in the bar sitting between Pierre von Shalburg and Chef Carlos, though she doubted he'd have to break up any fights. Von Shalburg had declared Chef Carlos's wine and shallot sauce a "triumph" and Chef Carlos himself a "certified culinary genius," and since Chef Carlos agreed with that assessment, they were getting along famously. Tony's finesse and charm had saved the night—maybe even the resort. She wasn't so sure she could have handled the stuffy, self-important critic nearly as well as her partner had.

She smiled at the uncommon turn the last few weeks had brought.

Tony was still working hard, while, for once, she didn't want to even think about work. She concentrated on her surroundings, the emotions trembling inside her body.

The day had been warm and sunny; the night had turned cool, with a brisk wind blowing off the Sound. The breeze blew her hair off her shoulders and stirred the hem of the red silk chemise she wore. The air teased the heated folds between her legs, and she leaned her head back, concentrating on absorbing the sensation. Since she knew their intimate relationship wouldn't last, she felt compelled to soak up every moment and pleasure she and Tony had left. She wouldn't allow herself to dwell on the end, or the feelings for him that seemed to deepen every moment they were together. How would she ever find the resolve to go back to being just friends?

She'd become addicted to him, she decided. Or, at least, to his touch. Why else would she be standing outside in revealing lingerie, waiting for him, her heart pounding in anticipation, her body damp with need?

She hadn't turned on the balcony lights, so she doubted anyone could actually see her. Still, she felt both self-conscious and seductive. Would he be surprised to find her like this?

She shivered in anticipation of the look in his eyes, the fevered touch of his hands. Her skin heating, she slid her palm along her throat, but her touch wasn't enough. She wanted him.

How much longer?

Leaning against the railing, she picked up her wineglass, rolling the cool crystal across her chest. Her nipples puckered against her gown. Moisture beaded along her inner thigh.

She pictured him—the broadness of his shoulders in his elegant suit coat, the gleaming black of his hair, the tanned column of his throat, his laugh, his scent—and her breathing quickened. She couldn't wait to touch him, have him touch her.

"Ches?"

Startled, she turned, glancing over her shoulder.

He stood in the doorway, his body shadowed by the night.

Her heart rate kicked up again, and she started toward him. He had to soothe this wild ache in her blood.

But he held up his hand. "Don't move." His gaze raked over her. "You're the most beautiful woman I've ever seen."

With Tony, that was saying a lot.

And his words, the expression in his eyes, added a new layer to the mood. There was quivering excitement, desire and wonder, but also something much deeper. He stared at her as if he'd never get tired of looking. As if there was something more between them than attraction and friendship.

That can't be, she thought, her breath clogging her throat. This feeling would go away. She'd exhaust her hunger for him, then her life would get back on course. The One would come charging into her life, and her heart would finally be satisfied.

Something about that picture didn't seem to gel, but she didn't dwell on her troubling thoughts.

Tony had started toward her.

He stalked forward, stripping off his jacket in the last few steps. "Turn back around," he said, embracing her from behind.

Her hips bumped the railing as he pressed his erection against her backside, and his breath rushed over her nearly bare shoulder.

"Do you taste as delicious as you look?" he asked softly against her skin.

She let her head fall back, and he pushed her hair aside, trailing kisses along her neck and nape. His hands slid over her hips, then her thighs, stroking the silk, working the chemise up higher and higher.

A breeze rushed over her, sending a chilling caress over her skin, the apex of her thighs, her bottom. Still kissing her neck and shoulders, Tony slid his hands around to her backside, squeezing lightly, then gliding down the back of her thighs.

She shuddered with need.

He pulled her back against him, groaning in her ear, his hands flexing against her hips. Her bare backside slid against the edge of his zipper.

She closed her eyes and fought to gain control of her breathing. The firm feel of his hands, the heat of his mouth, the silk gliding against her bare skin, they all rolled together in a maelstrom of erotic sensations.

Needy, with the coil of desire winding itself into a tight knot, she bumped her bottom against his hardness.

"Soon, *bella*," he said. "Soon."

Then he slid his hands around her thighs, his fingertips crawling toward her femininity.

She gripped the railing. She wanted him to stop teasing. She wanted his touch. Now. Intimately. Immediately.

Heat pulsed through her. Her senses stretched out as if they could draw him closer, intensify his touch, bring her the satisfaction and completion she craved.

When he finally drew his fingers through the damp heat between her legs, she sagged against him. She was fully under his control now, panting, spellbound. The pressure of his fingers sent delicious thrills through her body. The coil tightened. Her stomach muscles clenched.

He flicked his tongue across her earlobe as his fingers teased her flesh. His erection throbbed against her backside. When he sank his teeth into her earlobe, she exploded.

She gasped as the waves of pleasure rocked her, pulsing in powerful, rhythmic thrusts, leaving her blissfully drained.

As the last echoes of her climax rolled through her, she drew deep breaths, supporting her weight on the balcony railing. Then she whirled, thrusting her arms around his neck, pulling him close for a long, wet kiss.

"You do know how to thank a guy," he said when they came up for air.

She smiled, her gaze locking with his. "You bet I do." Then she jumped up, wrapping her legs around his hips to support herself.

He held her up beneath her thighs. "I've always liked aggressive women."

"Good, because I intend to have my wicked way with you."

His erection jerked against her. "Can't wait for that," he said as he walked them into the room, heading directly for the bedroom.

"How are von Shalburg and Chef Carlos?"

"Please, don't mention those two," he said, cupping the back of her head with his hand and easing her onto the mattress.

With her legs still wrapped around him, she absorbed the lovely sensation of his body weight pinning her down. "Just tell me they're still happy."

"Blissful." He trailed kisses along her jaw. "It's damn weird."

She angled her head to give him better access. "Peas in a pod. They're both difficult and moody."

He groaned. "And love to hear the sound of their own voices."

Trailing her hand through his thick hair, she turned her head to look at him. "You were really great today. I never could have handled von Shalburg as well as you did."

His brown eyes softened. "Yes, you could have. You know more about what goes on here, what needs to be done, than anybody."

"We make a great team."

"I guess we do."

A quiet moment passed while they stared into each other's eyes. Was he, too, wondering how long they could hope for this to last? As far as the resort was concerned, part of her was still waiting for him to tell her he'd had enough, that he'd support the project financially, but he didn't want to be involved with the day-to-day aggravations and commitments.

She didn't know if she could run things alone. She certainly didn't want to.

And now those sentiments were fast becoming personal. There, at least, she *knew* he'd soon tell her it was over.

He smoothed her hair back from her face. "Ah, Ches, we haven't made a mess of things, have we?"

"I'm not sure. Do you regret us sleeping together?"

"Definitely not. You?"

"No."

"I—" He looked away, then back. "I can't stop thinking about you, about us together. I didn't expect to feel like this."

Even as her heart did a leap of joy, her practical side warned that while he might feel something toward her, that something wasn't long-lasting. And that was a good thing. Her feelings were firmly of the temporary variety, too. She couldn't pretend or dream otherwise. Tony was committed to very little except being a free-wheeling bachelor. Forgetting that—for even a moment—could only lead to heartache. "I've thought about us together for a long time, and I still didn't anticipate feeling this—" she slid her hand down his chest, stopping with her palm over his heart "—close."

Panic filled his eyes. "What are we going to—"

She laid her finger over his lips. "We're going to enjoy each other and not think about tomorrow."

"You?" He raised one eyebrow. "You plan bathroom breaks."

"Tony! I do not."

He kissed the end of her nose. "I could get used to the wild and reckless side of you, though."

Relief filled her. She was very afraid that if they examined their feelings too closely, they'd both realize this relationship wasn't going anywhere and might not even be good for their long-standing friendship. She *was* wild and reckless with him, but when it was over she didn't want any regrets. She had him for a little while, and she intended to enjoy him.

"One of us is overdressed," she said, working the buttons on his shirt.

"Oh, well, we have to fix that."

In moments, she had the shirt off and her hands on the muscles rippling across his chest. "Mmm." She raised her head and pressed her lips to his skin, tasting his warmth, inhaling the spicy scent of him.

She loved his strength, both the rough and soft textures of his skin. She was fascinated by the way he reacted to her touch. Sometimes he flinched as if overwhelmed, other times he pushed into her touch, silently asking for more.

When she raked her fingernail across his nipple, he flinched. When she flicked her tongue across the same spot, he sank against her.

"Are you trying to drive me out of my mind?" he asked as she kissed her way up his throat.

"Absolutely."

Retaliating, he slid her chemise up her thighs and pressed his erection tightly between her legs. The ache Francesca thought she'd sated roared back to life. She angled her hips so the tip of him pressed against the entrance to her body. He still wore his pants, and the friction of the fabric against her bare skin gave her a sweet thrill.

He clutched a handful of red silk, rubbing it against her stomach. His breath was coming in short bursts. "Have I mentioned I really like red?"

She undid his belt buckle. "I'll wear it more."

"How many of these silky things do you have?"

"A dozen or so."

He groaned. "What—" He cut himself off, probably because she'd wrapped her hands around his hardness. "Uh, we can...talk about clothes later."

As he leapt off the bed and stripped out of his pants, she sat up, yanking her chemise over her head. She flung the silk beside the bed and grabbed the box of condoms from the bedside table. He briskly handled the task of protection, and in seconds he was looming over her, his erection brushing her stomach. He slid his hands along her arms, drawing them above her head, then he threaded his fingers through hers, folding their hands together.

The gesture struck her as extremely intimate, even comforting, something old lovers or a married couple, might do.

Yikes. Bad train of thought.

They weren't old lovers, would never be old lovers. And as for mar—

He brought his hands back down and placed his palms on the bed to support his weight, then he thrust inside her.

She gripped his shoulders as her body enveloped him. He held himself still for a moment, and his gaze met hers. Ridiculously, tears burned behind her eyes. She closed her eyes in defense. She couldn't let him in her heart.

Then he slid his lips against her cheek and began to move inside her.

The ache deep within her seemed more profound suddenly. She wanted completion, she wanted the sensual high, the kick of pleasure, but she was also afraid she wanted much more than that.

Their bodies slid together, sweat beading on their skin, breaths mingling. His warmth, the hard muscles of his body, rippled beneath her hands. She dug her fingers into his back as he pressed deeper. Her body trembled beneath his touch, needing more of him, yet knowing he was giving all and everything he had.

She crested over the rise, not with the explosion of last night, but with a tender passion that again brought tears to her eyes. As he followed her, one tear leaked out, trickling across her cheek.

She hoped he didn't see, wouldn't question.
She only knew she wanted him to be The One.
And he just wasn't.

WITH HIS FACE buried against Francesca's neck, Tony breathed deep and easy. He floated on a puffy cloud, all his thoughts and movements languorous. He lazily wrapped his hand around her hair, letting the silky brown locks slide through his fingers.

"Where's the music coming from?" she asked, sounding sleepy. She turned on her side, so they lay belly to belly.

"Hmm?"

"My ears are ringing. It sounds like music."

He smiled. "I can make them do it again." With his hand holding the back of her head, he pressed his lips to hers, sliding his tongue into her mouth, consuming the sweet, warm taste of her.

Her breasts were pressed against his chest, one long, bare leg hooked around his hip, and he figured he could stay in this position for the next decade or so, but then he also heard the music. It didn't sound like a romantic ballad. It sounded like "Brick House."

He bolted upright. "I'm gonna strangle the little dweeb."

"Who?"

Tony glared at the floor where his pants—and that damn phone—lay. "Von Shalburg, who else?"

"What's he— That's the *phone* ringing?"

Crawling to the end of the bed, Tony grabbed his pants and dumped the phone out of the pocket. "Mr. von Shalburg, how are you?" he somehow managed to say while still grinding his teeth together.

"I'm considerably well. Dinner was excellent. Your chef is something to be proud of."

As if Carlos was a trained poodle or a particularly fine Chianti. "Isn't he?"

"I'm afraid I'm in a bit of a quandary, though."

"No kidding." Tony glanced back at Francesca, who'd propped herself on her elbow. Her naked breasts called to him. Really, they did.

And he was really going to kick von Shalburg's ass the next time he saw him.

"You see, I have this weakness for chocolate..."

"Really?" Having a weakness for something much more important than chocolate, Tony flopped back onto the bed, and Francesca leaned over him, smiling, threading her fingers through the hair at his temple.

"...so, anyway, I need another chocolate mint."

"A mint?"

"A whole handful would be nice."

Tony stared briefly into the phone. "A whole—" He shook his head. Just get rid of him. "Okay, Mr. von Shalburg. We're here for you. They're coming right up."

He jabbed the end call button, then dialed housekeeping. "Mabel, I know what time it is, but I need a handful of chocolate mints to room—"

"Three twenty-eight."

"How did you ever guess?"

"I'm psychic."

Tony sighed. "Would you like to bear my children?"

"Hell, no. I want that fine Mercedes in the back parking lot."

"Deal." He ended the call, then turned off the stupid

phone, shoving it across the bed. As soon as he found a hammer, he was pounding that thing to dust.

Francesca trailed her finger down the center of his chest. "Sounds like I have a rival for your affections."

He kissed her chin. "You're probably going to lose, too. Have you seen Mabel's biceps?"

FRANCESCA ACCEPTED a chilled glass of champagne from Mark, who was walking around with a tray full at the wine and cheese party. She sent him a conspiratorial wink, since he was now part of her "Deal with von Shalburg" team.

Despite the fact that Pierre von Shalburg was a fussbudget of the first order, she still intended to get that great review for the resort. So this morning she'd brought in all her most valued employees for a strategy meeting. No matter how aggravating he became, they had to please him. And, if they did, she was throwing them one hell of a party on Sunday night.

As a result, she'd spent the day perfecting the plans for this reception, as well as peeping in on cooking demos and wine tours, checking on the chocolate supply and assuring Mabel that Tony was only kidding when he'd offered her his Mercedes. Their fussy critic seemed content, and he continued to compliment Carlos's culinary efforts, but as she well knew from his horribly-timed phone call last night, the dam could break at any moment.

With her and Tony running in separate directions all day, she'd had time to think about the way their relationship was progressing.

It wasn't.

Like it or not, her practical side had finally kicked in.

Two big problems loomed—she wasn't the kind of woman who could hold Tony's interest for long, and he wasn't The One.

She'd promised herself she was through with dead-end relationships, and here she was in one. She'd waited for what seemed like forever to have him, and now that she did, she wanted the strength to give him up. She was either totally nuts or way too rational.

Someone brushed her arm. She looked up to find a handsome, blond man staring down at her. "Great party," he said, then flashed her a toothpaste-commercial-perfect smile.

She met his gaze, waiting for the spark of electricity, the flash of inspiration. She felt nothing. She was glad he'd come to the party, but The One he most definitely was *not*. Where *was* that man?

Still, she had hostess duties. "Glad you're having a good time. I'm Francesca D'Arcy, one of the owners of Bella Luna."

Mr. Perfect Smile held out his hand. "I'm Beck Foreman."

He even sounded like a toothpaste commercial. He was cute in an I'm-the-ideal-male-specimen kind of way. She shook his hand and asked, "Are you staying with us? I don't recall your name from the guest list."

"No, I'm staying at Chateau Fontaine."

They'd advertised the party to non-Bella Luna guests, hoping they could draw people from other resorts and residents of the area. For a flat price, attendees could enjoy all varieties of the Galini family wines, as well as fruit, cheese and guitar entertainment. They'd decided to host the party on the back patio and around the pool.

"You must be Tony's partner," Beck said. When she nodded, he continued, "Great guy. He and I had a blast a couple of weekends ago."

"It's hard not to with Tony."

He grinned. "The man does have a way with the ladies."

"I bet the two of you were quite a pair."

He shrugged, no doubt used to women noticing him. His gaze drifted down her figure. "He didn't give me entirely enough details about you, though."

Flattered, but still not feeling even the slightest required tingle, Francesca sipped her champagne. "I'm more of the silent partner."

"Francesca, may I talk to you a minute?" Scowling, Tony stalked toward them.

Francesca met Tony's gaze. Their picky critic was no doubt running rampant again. She might need a lot more champagne after this.

Beck held out his hand to Tony. "Hey, buddy, I—"

"Later, okay?" Tony barely even glanced his friend's way. "I really need to talk to Francesca a minute."

Beck shrugged. "Yeah, sure," he said as he wandered away.

Francesca glared at Tony. "That was rude."

"You don't want to encourage Beck."

Already unnerved by Pierre von Shalburg's annoying presence and her concerns over the viability of her and Tony's relationship, Francesca's temper spiked. "I didn't think I was."

"He's too much of a player for you."

"A player."

"Runs with a real party crowd, lives off the family money and spends most of it chasing women."

Francesca raised her eyebrows. "Oh, well, I'm sure with somebody like that I'd be completely out of my element." She paused. "Though I seemed to be handling myself well enough with you."

"Me? I don't have anything—" He stopped, frowning. "I'm not a player."

"You want me to repeat your definition?"

Tony grabbed her arm and steered her away from the milling crowd. "This doesn't have anything to do with us. I'm just trying to protect you."

He'd been doing a lot of that recently, and for a split second she thought he might be jealous. They were currently sleeping together, and no guy would be thrilled to find his lover trying to get with another guy right in front of him, but then she remembered it hardly mattered if Tony's pride was affected. She wasn't interested in Beck. She wished she could be. But no, this morning she'd sprayed Tony's cologne between her breasts, needing some part of him to stay with her, knowing this was the only part of him she could have all to herself.

Even now, when she inhaled, she could catch a whiff of the spicy aroma.

But then, maybe the fact that he was standing two inches from her had something to do with that. She leaned toward him. She really liked that smell. Like him, it was hot, sexy...elusive.

Excuse me, Miss Weak-in-the-Knees? Do you recall recognizing two big relationship problems less than fifteen minutes ago?

But he looked so delicious. Black hair a bit shiny, as if the waves were still damp. Tan slacks that fell in perfectly tailored lines down his long legs. His white silk shirt showed off his bronzy skin.

His hand flexed on her arm. "Ches, please, that smoky eye thing drives me crazy."

She blinked, looking up at him. What in the world was she doing?

Being greedy, that's what. She wanted another night with him. And another.

Hussy.

Oh, shut up, she told her conscience. She'd fantasized about Tony for over ten years, and they still had a few more highlights to hit.

But they couldn't hit them at the wine and cheese party in front of all their guests. She stepped back from him. "Sorry. My mind wandered."

He smiled. "Wanna tell me where?"

She waggled her finger at him. "I think I'm still supposed to be mad at you. You were rude to Beck, and I don't need you playing overbearing bodyguard."

"Fine by me." He leaned close. "I don't want to guard your body, I want to touch it, stroke it...become part of it."

Francesca's body heated; her head spun. She gulped from her glass. "What about Beck?" she managed to ask.

"I'll apologize." He twined his finger around a long hair that had escaped her topknot. "If he means that much to you."

Okay, that *really* sounded like jealousy. But she'd *never* seen Tony jealous of anyone. And now he'd acted that way twice in the last three days. "He's a guest at our party," she said, not wanting to make anything of her suspicion. Even though the thought of him being jealous gave her a cheap thrill.

"Right. I'm going." He released her hair, then turned away, and Francesca breathed a sigh of relief.

She had to get control of herself. This party was about business.

He glanced back over his shoulder. "I think I saw strawberries on the fruit trays." His mouth lifted on one side. "Want some?"

Anticipation crawled down her spine. "If you're offering."

"Oh, I'm offering." His smiled flashed before he strode off.

That man ought to come with a red sticker plastered across his chest, she thought: Warning—Hazardous Material.

Mark swung by her—saving her from her lustful thoughts. "Ms. D'Arcy, you might want to chat up Mr. von Shalburg. He's looking bored."

"You really know how to put a woman off her champagne," she called softly after the waiter.

She polished off the last of her glass, then headed to the bar to get a fresh one before setting off in the critic's direction. He was standing alone at the far end of the pool, glancing around as if human existence on any level was beneath him. He was a critic, after all. And, therefore, a god.

"Mr. von Shalburg, how was your day?"

He offered her a brief smile. "Ah, Ms. D'Arcy, my day has been so-so. A little busier than I'd like. Wine tastings, cooking demonstrations, tours of the facility—it's all a bit much. You do want people to come for a *relaxing* weekend, don't you?"

She ground her teeth. "Of course. I noticed several people sat on the porch and played cards after lunch. The demos and other activities are optional."

"And then the pool invites you to endlessly bake your body like a steak on a grill, doesn't it? That's relaxing for some, I suppose."

"It would seem so."

Von Shalburg gestured with his wineglass. "Your wines are something to be proud of, though. Joe Galini has cultivated his reputation and his vintages well."

If he expected her to ramble on about how much better the resort was than the Galini wines, he was very mistaken. Joe had spent fifteen years adding to his impeccable European reputation as a winemaker. Bella Luna was, in essence, simply an extension and support of that effort. No matter how successful the resort became, it would always exist to support the wines.

"Yes, he has."

"He appeared briefly when we toured the vineyards earlier."

He was digging. For dirt, or just background for his review? "He works as a partner with Tony and I. We run the resort; he runs the winery."

"Tony Galini has only recently come into the business, I understand."

"No." She cut her gaze in Tony's direction. "He's helped Joe with the harvest every year. He's been part of the decision-making process for quite a while. He's just now decided to take the business in a new, dynamic direction."

Von Shalburg raised his glass to her. "Excellent answer, Ms. D'Arcy. You managed to leave out each and every detail that would lead anyone to believe Mr. Galini has been happily living off his trust fund for the last twenty-nine years, partying in the New York clubs until the wee hours, romancing every female in a skirt."

It took every practical brain cell she had in her body to keep from dumping the contents of her champagne glass over that horrible man's head. Tony might not be Donald Trump, but he was doing just fine with the business. How dare von Shalburg imply otherwise?

She bared her teeth and leaned toward him. "Tony's commitment over the last several months has been invaluable. As for this weekend, I'd say his behavior has been close to saint-like. He's carried around a cell phone, making himself available every moment to accommodate your slightest whim. He's had white, fluffy towels, liquor and chocolates delivered at all hours of the day and night. Frankly, I'm surprised and disappointed that a man of your reputation would pay heed to rumors that have nothing whatsoever to do with this resort."

Francesca whirled, then stalked away, her breath heaving. She'd just told off the most influential critic on the east coast. He'd hate her. He'd trash Bella Luna. But, dammit, he wasn't going to talk about Tony that way. Regardless of their current relationship, she and Tony had been, and would always be, friends. Besides, now she had no doubts about whether or not he had the dedication to make this resort work.

They *would* be a success.

And not because Pierre von Shalburg deemed it so, but because they'd worked hard to make their dreams happen. Personally, they might be wrong for each other. They might have different goals. But as business partners they were the best.

Suddenly, he was in front of her, grabbing her arms, pulling her toward him. "Ches? What's wrong? Are you okay? What happened?"

Hot air heaved in and out through her teeth. "We're going to get a bad review from von Shalburg."

"Why? What happened? I sent him so many chocolates last night I'm surprised he didn't overdose."

She drew a deep, shaky breath. "I told him off."

"You—" He stopped, his eyes widening in shock. "Ches, we've driven ourselves crazy for this."

"Not anymore. He's not worth it."

"You've spent the last two weeks telling me he was worth anything."

Pretty sure steam was shooting out of her ears, she glanced up at him. "Not this."

11

TONY TRIED not to panic. Von Shalburg was his responsibility. He'd promised Francesca and Joe he could handle the critic. Francesca had to be exaggerating. The review couldn't have gone down the toilet that fast.

What could have happened that would make her go over the edge? Francesca had worked harder than anybody to make Bella Luna a success. Nothing could have forced her to compromise that. Nothing.

Unless—

"Did he come on to you?"

"No."

"Did he try to touch you?"

She gripped his wrist. "No. Nothing like that. He just said some things he shouldn't have."

"About you."

She sighed, her gaze flicking to his. "No, about you."

A little of Tony's panic ebbed. "What things?"

"He intimated you only recently got interested in the family business."

"I did."

"The harvest—"

"Was once a year. Not much of an involvement."

"But he...he acted like you'd done nothing with your life until now. Like you'd mooched off your family and—"

"You have to admit my life lacked direction until recently." He paused, ignoring a pang of hurt before continuing. "You said so yourself not ten minutes ago when you accused me of being a player."

Francesca sank onto a lounger beside the pool. "I've been an idiot."

Tony knelt next to her. "No, I have. All the things you and von Shalburg said about me are true. I didn't have goals, and I went into this resort project without much direction or commitment."

She shook her head. "Still, I wasn't very nice earlier." Her gaze searched his. "You have my respect, Tony. Always. You know that, don't you?"

He focused on her face but tried not to show how much her words meant to him. "Of course."

"Von Shalburg didn't have the right to judge the way you've led your life," she said. "And neither did I."

"You were worried about me, I guess."

She reached for his hand, threading her fingers through his. He wondered if she remembered when he'd touched her the same way last night, just before their bodies had joined. The memory had his heart racing.

"That was part of it," she said. "But mostly I was just imposing my own goals on you. You're different than me, Tony. I shouldn't have tried to change you, mold you into *my* version of a business executive."

"You haven't. I might have changed over the last several months, but I've become my own kind of businessman. One I like and can live with." He smiled. "I'm actually pretty proud of myself." He might not have earned anyone else's respect, but he had his and Francesca's. And Joe's, too, if the pleased smile and wink he'd seen earlier during the winery tour was any indication. He didn't care about anyone else.

"Your commitment to helping me with the review has been terrific. Not that I've been too appreciative." She bit her lip. "I wouldn't blame you if you wanted out of this partnership."

She looked so miserable, he wanted to pull her into his arms. He settled for squeezing her hand and sitting next to her on the lounger. This responsibility stuff was hell on his libido. "I don't. I'm not going anywhere. I know I've complained a lot, but I like what I'm doing. I like...working."

She blinked.

"And look at you," he continued. "You protected me instead of the resort." Which he was still having trouble picturing. Bella Luna meant more to her than anything.

"I did, didn't I? That's very progressive of me." Smiling, she angled her head. "You know, I told myself earlier we were going to make it, and now I'm saying it out loud. No matter what Pierre von Shalburg says about us or our resort, we're going to make this work."

Tony placed a kiss against her wrist. "Of course we are, *bella.*"

Her gaze turned smoky, and he was acutely aware of her thigh, exposed by the pale yellow sundress she wore, pressed along the length of his leg. This party was supposed to be their big chance to schmooze new clients for the resort—something part of him craved, while another part couldn't care less about.

"Thank you for defending me," he said softly.

"Thank you for holding me together."

The intimate moment called for a much more personal setting than the pool deck, but again the professional aspect intruded. The innate seducer in Tony chafed under the restriction. But then, he'd never been much of a rule-follower anyway. Surely he could find a way to play host and further his need to be with Francesca at the same time.

"We've got to get through this party. And dinner. And the first set of the band. But after that..." He stroked the back of his hand across her cheek. "You're mine."

Her eyes flashed. "All night?"

"Every minute."

They could have gotten together years ago, he realized. Why had he been wasting his time with Mandy, Sandy and Candy? He'd never felt as close to anyone as he did to Francesca. Could he really have maintained a sexual relationship and a friendship with her all this time? Did he really have that kind of dedication in him?

But then a few months ago, he wouldn't have thought he had enough commitment in him for the resort either, and look where that had led. He just wished he knew what to do about her, his growing feelings for her. Part of him sensed they couldn't ebb along in this affair. He'd done that for way too long in his relationships. Decisions would have to be made.

Her fingers crawled along his thigh. "I missed you today."

Tomorrow. He could make decisions tomorrow.

He captured her hand, sliding his thumb across the back. "I'm here, whenever you need me."

She squeezed his hand. "But barely close enough to touch."

He met her gaze—the smoke was brilliantly evident. "Surely we don't have to touch for you to realize how much I want you?"

"No," she whispered, "but that doesn't make it any easier to resist you."

"What would you do if you could touch me?"

Glancing sideways briefly, she licked her lips, then directed her gaze back to his. "I'd unbutton your shirt and draw my hand down your bare chest."

His pulse throbbed against her palm. His body hardened like a rock.

"Then I'd wrap my other hand around your neck, comb my fingers through your hair...and pull you toward me for a kiss."

"Slow or hard?"

"Whichever you want."

Oh, hell. Tony gripped the lounge chair. Resistance was pretty much a lost cause. He *had* to touch her. How much could he get away with in this crowd?

He glanced around, only to see Mark a few feet away talking to a gray-haired couple and pointing in Tony's direction.

Not a whole lot. The couple was walking toward them.

"Aren't you Tony Galini?" the woman asked as he rose to shake both their hands.

"Yes." He pulled Francesca up beside him. "And this is my partner, Francesca D'Arcy."

"Your Uncle Joe and I are old friends."

"Really? What do you think of the resort?"

The woman went on to give glowing remarks about the resort, the winery and the food. Tony threw himself into concentrating on the conversation, though he was acutely aware of Francesca standing beside him. Her side brushed his twice. He could feel the heat of her body.

Or maybe that was just his own body roaring with flames—from the inside out.

After Joe's friends, other people came and went. He and Francesca wound up separated, and he took the opportunity to apologize to Beck. He used the old "working too hard, stressed out" excuse people had used on him many times. Work had some advantages. Go figure.

When a slinky redhead distracted Beck, Tony set off in search of Francesca. He found her at the far end of the pool, accepting a glass of ice water from the bartender.

Standing directly behind her, he slid his finger down her spine. Her hand shook, sloshing a bit of water over the sides. "A successful party," he said, his casual tone contrasting with the tightness invading his body, the desire rolling through his stomach.

She thanked the bartender, then glanced at him over her shoulder. "Personally, I'm a little hot."

On that note, his erection pulsed, and he begged the bartender for a tall, icy glass of water.

Drinks in hand, they walked away from the bar, Francesca in front of him. As he gulped his water, the low back on her sundress distracted him, and he got an idea. "Stand in front of me," he said close to her ear.

"Why?"

"You'll see," he said, walking around her so they both faced the pool. This way, they could stand like sentries and appear as though they were actually interested in the party, but he could still indulge his desire to meet skin-to-skin.

As she sipped her water, he laid his hand—the one that had been wrapped around his cold glass—against her lower back.

She jumped. "Tony!"

He chuckled in her ear. "You said you were hot."

She turned, glaring at him. "I've had about all the jolts I can take today, thank you."

"How is good ole von Shalburg?"

"I wouldn't know." She flushed. "I've been avoiding him."

That wasn't like Francesca at all. She pretty much met people and situations head-on. But then von Irritating could drive a saint to act unreasonably. He'd sent a bow-wrapped bottle of Dewar's to the critic's room. Maybe the bribe would encourage him to overlook his and Francesca's argument.

He urged her back around, then slid his fingers across her back. "I can't wait to get you naked," he said in her ear.

Her breathing quickened. "When?"

"Right after the band's first set."

"Not sooner?"

Swallowing hard, he gripped her waist. "Sooner?"

"How about between dinner and the band starting?"

Dear heaven, was there any greater aphrodisiac to a man than a woman who wanted him? "I think my schedule's clear then," he managed to say, though desire nearly choked him.

"Can we really make it till then?"

"I'm not sure." And he really wasn't. His responsibility as a resort owner was under serious duress. He wanted to throw Francesca over his shoulder and run off with her to some distant beach, where eating coconuts, drinking champagne and making love would be his biggest goals.

They *could* go. After that irritating critic left, he could whisk Francesca away for a few days of pleasure. Hell, *after* he left? They could go *now*. No one would miss them. They had a capable staff. Everything would be fine if they just slunk off—

No. What if everything wasn't fine? What if Pierre von Shalburg demanded something ridiculous from Mabel in housekeeping? Who would be her buffer? What if he insulted Derrick the bellhop? Or Carlos? Or Kerry?

Oh, God. He *had* become a responsible business owner.

He slid his hand up Francesca's spine one last time. "Let's make the rounds again."

Over her shoulder, she looked at him, desire evident in her eyes. "Now?"

"Horrible timing, I know, but shouldn't we support our staff?"

"Of course, but— Are you sure this is what you really want?"

He raked his gaze over her luscious body, thinking

about the delights beneath her clothes. He closed his eyes, the only way he could say what had to be said. "Yes."

"This is kind of weird—you pulling me back to our responsibilities."

"Definitely." He urged her forward, his hand hot against her bare back. "Let's go now, before I change my mind."

They survived the party—just barely in Tony's estimation. Then they had dinner with Joe and a group of his friends. His uncle, Tony reflected, had run a respected, successful business for many years, and he'd made countless friends in the process. Tony hoped the same could be said about him in twenty years.

After dinner, he and Francesca made the rounds through the tables of guests. Everyone seemed pleased, though there were a few comments about the hot tub being too crowded, the food too spicy—or not spicy enough.

As he finished his walk through the restaurant, Tony searched for Francesca. He asked waiters, the maître d', the kitchen staff. No one had seen her.

They had a date for...pleasure. Where could she have gone?

Visions of finding her in that red silky chemise in his room last night danced through his memory. Maybe she'd gone upstairs. He trotted up all three flights rather than taking the elevator and arrived at her room grinning and out of breath.

Francesca met him at the door, wearing a smile and another chemise—a sapphire-blue one with a plunging, eye-popping neckline—and carrying a martini. "Hi, honey. Hard day at work?"

He wrapped his arm around her waist, lifting her as he stalked inside the room. "Not anymore."

12

FRANCESCA WOKE, warm and content.

Tony's bare chest was pressed against her back, his arm flung over her side, his hand across her stomach. His deep, even breathing filled her ears. Smiling, she covered his hand with hers, and he pulled her tighter against him. She could lie here for the next several years. Maybe even—

Her heart jumped. She couldn't do anything of the kind.

She was a temporary diversion in Tony's love life. He wouldn't hang around much longer. He never did. And though she loved him—as her friend, her long-time pal—if she spent one more night, one more hour, hell, one more minute entangled intimately with him, that friendly love would become real love. The kind you don't escape, talk yourself out of, or forget. Ever.

And knowing he'd break her heart, the resolve she'd searched for yesterday rolled through her. She closed her eyes for a moment, fighting against the hollow ache in her stomach.

Then she slid out of the bed, showered and dressed, all the while her conscience convincing her this was the right thing to do. She couldn't keep doing this, sharing her body and pretending no other part of her was involved. Pretty soon, she'd fall too hard to pull away.

She couldn't try to hang on to him when he moved on to another woman. She wouldn't do that to herself—or him.

She had to go. The One—her love-at-first-sight life partner—was out there waiting for her, and she needed to get serious about finding him. She hadn't really tried up to now. Had she ever used one of those Internet websites? Gone speed dating? She'd dated a few guys through recommendations from friends, but had she really told her circle of buddies that she wanted a permanent relationship? No. She'd chickened out on that. Because she'd been too focused on her career? Because she was afraid to take that step?

Or because she was holding out for Tony?

As she walked slowly out of the bathroom toward the bed, she took a moment to absorb the sight of his dark head against the crisp, white sheets. Tears already burning the backs of her eyes, she nudged his shoulder. "Tony, we have to talk."

Tony buried his face into his pillow. "Mmm. Later."

"We have to talk now."

Before I chicken out. Before I cry hysterically, forget all my hopes and dreams and goals.

Finally, his eyes popped open. He wrapped his hand around her wrist and tugged her down to the bed, kissing her with head-spinning thoroughness. "Morning," he said, his voice still husky with sleep.

"Good morning," she said, breathing deeply to slow her heartbeat. "I need to talk to you."

His lips curved upward as he sat up, holding her against his bare chest. "Later. I know a much better way to start the morning."

She laid her palm on his chest. "No, Tony." She pulled out of his arms and stood. "We need to talk now."

He angled his head, his surprised gaze sweeping over her, as if just now realizing she was fully dressed and far from being in a romantic mood.

She watched him, the words she had to say frozen in her throat. He was so beautiful with his tousled hair and tanned, bare shoulders. He meant the world to her.

He ran his hand through his hair. "It's over, isn't it?"

Even in her grief, she was grateful for his insight. "Yes." She linked her hands in front of her, clenching them tightly. "We can't go on this way. It won't last, and I promised myself I wouldn't get involved in relationships like this anymore. I need to get my life and goals back on track."

His dark gaze flicked to hers. "You want The One—your Mr. Right."

"Yes."

"And I'm not him."

Was that a question, or a statement? Francesca quashed the hope that he might be asking. She sat on the edge of the bed. "I know you're not ready to settle down. You may never be. There's nothing wrong with that. It's just not for me. I want what my parents have—love, a lifelong relationship, maybe even kids and a house in the suburbs someday."

"I know," he said quietly. "And the biggest commitment I've ever made to a woman is making dinner plans at eight."

She wanted to reach for his hand, pull him into her arms, but she was frankly afraid to touch him. Her resolve shook deep within her, and she feared it breaking free. "We're friends and business partners. I want to keep it that way."

His eyes were bleak as he looked up at her. "But things are never going to be the same, *bella.*"

Her heart stopped, then started again at a relentless pace. "Yes, they will. We're friends. We're always going to be friends."

He shook his head. "But not friends like before. We know too much about each other now. I know where to touch you to make you moan. I know your eyes go smoky when you're aroused. I can't just pretend I don't know that."

"But we agreed," she sputtered out. "You said—"

"I was an idiot." He thrust his hand through his hair. "I've been friends with ex-lovers before, but..." He shook his head. "But somehow this is different."

This can't be. I can't lose you completely. "It'll just take time."

He looked away. "Maybe."

He actually seemed sad. *Tony?* She certainly hadn't expected this reaction. He'd loved and left so many women she hadn't expected much more from him than a *Hey, Ches it was fun. What's for dinner?*

She started to reach for his hand, then pulled back. If she touched him, she was afraid of what she might do or promise. But she couldn't deny the feeling that something precious was slipping through her fingers faster than water through a colander. "Tony—"

"It was fun, though," he said suddenly, and a fake, bright smile passed across his face. "For a few days anyway."

She forced her own smile and prayed she was right about things getting back to normal with time. "Yeah." Numb and sick to her stomach, she rose and started across the room. "I'm going to head downstairs, check on things."

Just as she reached the bedroom doorway, she heard his voice behind her.

"Ches, how will you know when you find him?"

Drawing a deep breath, pushing past the sharp stab of pain in her lungs, she glanced over her shoulder. "I'll just know."

I hope.

TONY PRESSED harder on the Mercedes' gas pedal. He had to get away from that place, away from her. Barbados sounded good.

If he drove far enough, fast enough, could he forget the smoky blue in her eyes, the silky feel of her skin? Could he dismiss her smile and her laugh? Could he forget how she'd held the resort—and him—together?

The pain in his chest said otherwise.

He'd never again wake beside her. He'd never feel her bare body alongside his.

Why did those realities hurt so much? Why couldn't he shrug this off? He'd known it was coming. He'd known it couldn't last. Nothing did. And he liked his life that way.

She'd even made things easy for him—breaking off their affair before he'd have been forced to. But instead of feeling relief and anticipation about his next lovely lady, he couldn't seem to draw a deep enough breath.

As the car bounced over the bumpy road, the landscape rolled by, the afternoon sun glared through the windshield, but he felt no better. He clenched the steering wheel until his knuckles whitened. Nothing had changed. Nothing inside. Nothing that mattered.

There was only one thing to do—go back to work. He had to get von Shalburg out of the resort and think of ways to attract new guests, especially if the critic turned out to be as big a jerk as Tony thought he was and gave them a lousy review. The pool party he'd planned for next weekend would be a good first start—for him and for business.

He'd concentrate on the resort. He'd stay busy, force these feelings to stop. Life would be back to normal in no time.

He'd whipped the car around and was halfway back before he realized he wasn't running away.

All his life he'd avoided conflict, skirted responsibility. But he'd found direction and purpose in his life. The opportunity at the resort had given him goals, which Joe and Francesca had helped him accomplish. And now he was committed to his own success.

He could be committed to Francesca, too. So why had he let her sit beside him and end the most important relationship he'd ever had?

She was yours for a little while. What more do you want?

More. A lot more.

Back at the resort, he stalked through the lobby, intending to find Francesca, but he asked the front desk for his messages first.

The message on top had him barely holding back a scream. Pierre von Shalburg wanted to see him. Damn. He didn't have time to deal with the critic from hell.

TONY ENTERED von Shalburg's suite at the critic's invitation and found his bags packed and sitting just inside the door.

Thank God.

The man himself lounged on the sofa dressed in a navy blue suit—complete with matching three-button vest—sipping an amber-colored liquid from a crystal glass. He smiled as Tony approached. "Ah, Mr. Galini, I'm glad you had time to visit."

Tony resisted the urge to roll his eyes. "Always—for my favorite guest."

To his shock, von Shalburg burst out laughing. Rubbing the tears from his eyes, he said, "What a pro you are. I'm impressed. Real impressed."

Tony angled his head. Von Shalburg's voice sounded different. Twangy. "I'm so glad," he said, wondering if his chest pains and inability to breathe properly had also affected his hearing. Maybe he was having a heart attack.

Would Francesca come to his funeral and cry? Maybe she'd wear that short black dress she'd worn to the Chateau's bar.

"Have a seat," von Shalburg said, indicating the club chair next to him.

If this was going to be a synopsis of the "Run, Don't Walk From the New Resort Called Bella Luna" review von Shalburg was planning, Tony didn't want any part of the conversation. But he kept his emotions in check and dropped into the chair.

Von Shalburg took a sip from his glass, then leaned back, his gaze meeting Tony's. "You passed, bubba. I had my doubts a few times, especially in the beginning, but you pulled it off."

Tony raised his eyebrows. *Bubba?* "Passed what?"

"Me." All but popping from his vest with excitement, von Shalburg leaned forward. "If you can deal with pompous, nitpicky me, you can deal with anybody. I think you'll be a hootin' success."

"A hootin'—" Tony shook his head.

Von Shalburg held out his hand. "I don't believe I properly introduced myself. Hoyt Ewing. Pierre von Shalburg is my *nom de plume.*"

Instinctively, Tony shook the man's hand, still staring at him without understanding. Von Shalburg was really a Texan named Hoyt?

"Sorry to hoodwink ya. I like having a regular life outside of my job. And, to be frank, how many folks would be interested in Hoyt Ewing's opinion? On beer and barbecue, maybe, but definitely not wine and high-falutin' resorts." He winked. "I'm from Alabama, by the way. Not all the Ewings come from Dallas."

Stunned, Tony rose, shoving his hand through his hair. "You *are* the Pierre von Shalburg who writes for *A Vino?*"

"Oh, yeah. Made a real name for myself. It's a big kick."

"And the act?"

"The publisher of the magazine is a friend of my mama's. He knew about my qualifications—Culinary Institute of America graduate, master sommelier, world traveler—but I couldn't seem to get anywhere in the culinary industry. Lots of people told me to go to diction school and get rid of my accent. But how could I do that to Mama? My heritage?"

"I'm guessing no one else knows about this," Tony said, still somewhat shell-shocked. "Why me?"

"Well, bubba, believe it or not, that's where our roads of destiny meet, so to speak. You grew up privileged, with moneyed, jet-setting parents and a trust fund, so most people assume you're shallow and spoiled, right?"

Tony rolled his shoulders back. He'd be the first to admit he wasn't the deepest person in the world, but he certainly wasn't the stereotypical version of a trust-fund baby either. "The small-minded ones do anyway."

Hoyt raised his hand. "Have to admit I was one of those. So, at first, I had my doubts about you and this resort. A rich, club-hopping playboy—even if he is the nephew of a respected winemaker—isn't exactly the ideal resort owner. I expected a flashy place with little substance."

"But you've changed your mind?"

"You betcha. See, that's what people thought of me—but kinda in reverse. Because I have a Southern accent and grew up eating fried chicken and grits rather than eating spa food and drinking expensive wines, everybody assumed I couldn't possibly learn about those things, much less review them."

"So you invented Pierre von Shalburg," Tony said slowly.

"I took a few acting classes, which focused on diction, but I didn't change me, I just created Pierre. And after a bit, I realized the advantages of the act—not just for my column's respectability, but also for my own life. I could come and go as I pleased as Hoyt and still be the stuffy taskmaster as Pierre.

"And I learned that being picky and—eventually—a real pain in the ass had its advantages. I began to think of my special visits to hotels and resorts as tests. This is a tough business, and I can't have the great places folding up their tents because customers are difficult. People are looking for an escape, a vacation from the real world, and they have a right to expect quality for their money. I decided I'd be the most difficult customer, so if the reviewee survived my visit, and I thought highly of the food, wine and atmosphere, I could make reasonably sure of both their success and mine."

"That's really slick."

Hoyt beamed. "I thought so."

"And you're trusting me with this?"

"I like you, bubba. And I respect your dedication, especially when I know from experience you had plenty of people discouraging you from your predestined path. I trust you with my secret. No question."

Strangely honored, Tony continued to pace beside the chair. He'd earned more respect. Working hard—even sacrificing occasionally—could be...what had Hoyt said? A big kick.

If only Francesca could see him now. His stomach was in knots because of her, but this revelation by Hoyt eased at least some of his worries. They really had succeeded. They'd known they could do it without the favorable review, but Tony couldn't help the burst of pride at what they'd accomplished. He couldn't wait to tell Sonny his betting pool was all washed up.

"Hey," Hoyt said, "also got to congratulate you on finding such a qualified and loyal partner in Ms. D'Arcy. Classy lady. In fact, the only time I pushed her button was yesterday when she defended you at the wine tasting. She was dying to lay into me, but didn't. That's professionalism."

"Yeah," Tony said, distracted by the mention of Francesca's name. What was she doing now? Was she as miserable as him, or had she shrugged him off without another thought?

"Nice to have someone that...faithful by your side, I expect."

"Mmm."

"You like her...for a partner?"

Given the morning's parting, the word *partner* suddenly had a whole new meaning. The One—aka Mr. Perfect—would no doubt be smotheringly loyal to Francesca. But, hey, he could be loyal, too. He could try it, at least. "Oh, yeah. She's great."

In the process of sipping his drink, Hoyt gestured with his glass. "You two have a great thing going. Friends a long time?"

Tony nodded.

"That explains the balance. And the chemistry."

Tony didn't bother to deny the obvious. "Do you really think I can make this work?"

"Yep. You didn't try to kill me or kick me out, did you?"

"I wanted to."

Hoyt waved this away. "But you didn't. Let me tell you something about the hotel and restaurant business I expect you've already figured out, but it bears repeatin'—it ain't for the faint of heart. It takes guts, hard work, brains and commitment. And you got 'em."

Sighing, Tony shook his head. "Doesn't feel that way."

Hoyt's sharp gaze met his. "Are we talkin' about somethin' more personal than resort management now?"

Tony considered the idea that he was having a conversation about his most intimate and important relationship with Pierre/Hoyt.

Weird? Definitely.

But, hell, he wasn't exactly doing a bang-up job on his own.

"Yes," Tony said finally, "we're talking about something more personal."

"I figured." Hoyt looked at him over the rim of his glass. "What were you doing that night when I called about the mints, by the way?"

Tony recalled slick, naked bodies. "Something much more important than talking to you about mints."

Von Shalburg winked. "I'll bet. So what went wrong in two days?"

"She dumped me."

Shaking his head, Hoyt rose. "This calls for a drink."

"I'm not really a Dewar's fan."

Hoyt crinkled up his face. "Me either. I just ordered it because it was the only one you didn't have. I'm strictly a Jack Daniel's man."

Tony coughed. "Uh, I'm more of a martini man."

"Humph. Figures." But Hoyt started building the martini. "You really ought to get a more manly drink, Galini."

"I'd like to keep my esophagus in one piece, thanks."

"Wuss."

"Snob."

Smiling, the two men toasted each other.

HALFWAY THROUGH his second martini, Tony decided Hoyt was a great guy. The critic was now in the process of summarizing all Tony had told him about the last few months. "So, you started out wanting to prove to your uncle that you could succeed, which you've done—especially after my kick-ass review appears in a few weeks. You've got goals and a new direction in your life. And yesterday you realized you've earned your uncle's and Francesca's respect. Keeping that up will be a cinch for you, since I've already explained you've got all the commitment and tenacity you need to succeed."

Tony propped his feet on the coffee table, deciding Hoyt was even craftier than his alter ego. "That was an ego booster for me, wasn't it?"

Hoyt cut his gaze in Tony's direction. "Maybe. But true, so it hardly matters." He cleared his throat, then continued. "You said Francesca wants The One—a real lifelong commitment with a man she can respect. But the physical part of your relationship..."

"Is better than great."

"There's a plus."

"Don't forget that business of her defending me to you. She might have been professional, but she still took a big risk, knowing you might have given us a bad review."

"Oh, yeah."

Tony fingered the rim of his glass. "That's interesting, don't you think?"

"Mmm." Hoyt was silent a moment, then he added, "So, she respects you, defends you, is devoted to you *and* had a crush on you for eleven years."

His brain a little fuzzy, Tony nodded. "That sounds about right."

"You're hurt and upset that she dumped you. You haven't thought about another woman in weeks. You've been snarling and jealous every time another man comes within ten feet of her. *And* you trust and respect her like no one else."

He thought the snarling and jealous part was a bit much, but that was pretty much the gist of things. "Uh-huh."

Hoyt set his glass on the table with a bang. "You love her. She loves you. So tell her already."

Tony stiffened. "Don't be ridiculous."

"Ridiculous, maybe, but I'm not blind. *You're* The One for her."

Tony was sure he'd been punched. "I am *not*."

Hoyt jumped to his feet. "Are so."

Tony's heart threatened to jump from his chest. The man was completely crazy. He wasn't in love. Couldn't be. No chance.

Just because he didn't want to draw another breath without her next to him didn't mean he loved her.

No way.

Hoyt threw up his hands, shaking his head as he started toward the door. "Look, I gotta get back to the city to file my story."

Tony rose, a bit unsteadily—and not necessarily because of the drinks. "I'll call the bellhop."

"And a cab, too. I need to get to the train station." Shoving his hands in his pockets, Hoyt glared up at Tony. "Come to your senses, bubba. When I call you next week, you'd better have good news for me."

Ha! He was actually supposed to listen to relationship advice from *Hoyt?* No way. No chance.

Saying nothing, he called for a bellhop, then walked with Hoyt downstairs. He felt as though he'd made a new friend this afternoon, but he was really going to have to set the man straight about this love thing.

The trouble was, Tony couldn't think of a single argument.

And that scared the hell out of him.

After seeing Hoyt off, he wandered back into the lobby and heard singing from the bar. What was going on in there?

Half the hotel employees, plus Francesca, Uncle Joe and Fin, the Chateau's manager, were gathered around the bar, singing what sounded like "Finnegan's Wake," which was, naturally, sung at Irish wakes.

Fin, though, looked perfectly healthy to him.

As the song died away, they all raised their various glasses as Joe announced, "To hell with him," then downed the contents of a shot glass.

Tony raised his eyebrows. Obviously, the "Deal with von Shalburg" team was blowing off a little steam.

"Tony!" Joe cried as he spotted him in the doorway.

Sitting next to Joe, Francesca turned her head. Their gazes met briefly. She look apprehensive, almost sad.

That matched his own miserable mood just perfectly. But he had to talk to her, find a way past their differences. He couldn't imagine his life this way—always feeling regretful when he saw her. As though he was missing out on something wonderful.

On the other side of Francesca, Fin slid his arm around her waist and said something in her ear.

Tony's whole body went rigid. His jaw locked; his fists clenched. He envisioned ripping Fin's arm from its socket—slowly. He took a step forward, fully intending to do just that when the realization hit him.

I love her.

No doubts. No questions. No kidding.

He was in love—all the way, forever after. Hoyt had been right. This was very simple—he loved her, she—

Oh, hell. This wasn't simple at all. He had no idea how she felt about him. Dumping him couldn't have been a good sign.

But Hoyt had been right about his feelings. Maybe he was right about hers. Maybe she just didn't *know* she loved him. Well, he'd be the first one to tell her.

"Is he gone?" Joe asked suddenly.

Dragging his gaze from Fin's hand on Francesca's back, Tony stared at his uncle. "Who?"

"Pierre von Shalburg."

"Oh, him. Yeah." Tony walked slowly toward Francesca. He needed to get himself under control so he could talk to her calmly. And as much as he'd like to do so over Fin's unconscious body, he didn't think Francesca would approve.

"So what did he say about the review?" Joe asked.

Everyone—from Derrick the bellhop to Mabel in housekeeping—looked at him expectantly.

Tony continued his purposeful walk toward Francesca. "Oh, it'll be out in a few weeks."

"How bad is it going to be?" Francesca asked quietly.

In the process of absorbing the lovely, curvy sight of her in a cream-colored pantsuit, Tony had to haul his brain back to the topic of Hoyt and his review. "Not bad. Good. He's crazy about the place." He picked up Fin's arm by the wrist and removed it from Francesca's body. "Sorry, pal. I need my partner for a moment."

Fin gave him a quizzical look. "Sure."

Tony grabbed Francesca's hand and helped her off the stool. "I need to talk to you," he said, his gaze fixed on hers, his heart pounding nervously, anticipating the words he'd say to her, the look in her eyes when their meaning sank in.

"Crazy about the place?" she asked, planting her feet as he tried to draw her away from the bar. "I thought he was royally ticked off."

"No, he's all right. We impressed him actually." He tugged her forward, and she fell against him. He tried not to groan at the feel of her body pressed against his. "I've got something important to talk to you about."

"More important than the review?"

"Yes." He pulled her along beside him as he walked away from the others.

Now, where could they go? The bar was too loud, the lobby too public. He hadn't thought this whole thing out too clearly. All he knew was that he had to tell her about his feelings, had to know how she felt about him. Surely, she felt the same. And if she didn't, he'd find out why, then change her mind.

He wound up taking her out the back door. Guests lounged by the pool, but the patio was deserted for the moment.

Suddenly nervous, he combed his fingers through his hair. He needed the right words, the right tone, the right mood.

"What do you want, Tony?" she asked, crossing her arms over her chest.

Okay, so he hadn't set the right mood.

He stood in front of her, drew a deep breath, then said, "I love you."

Francesca's jaw dropped. "Don't be ridiculous."

Tony was pretty sure he'd been here before, but shook off the sense of déjà vu. "And you love me."

"No, I don't."

His heart plummeted. It had been a shot in the dark. "You don't?"

"Well, no, I—" Her gaze searched his. "You love me?"

"More than anything."

She looked skeptical. "Since when?"

"I'm not sure I know the exact moment it happened. I only realized it myself a few minutes ago."

"When?"

"When I walked into the bar and saw Fin touching you."

"And, bang! You think you love me."

"That's pretty much how it went." His gaze pierced hers. "And I don't think I love you, I know I do."

"Tony, this is…" She rubbed her temples. "Well, unbelievable. You have to realize how completely you've caught me off guard."

He drew her into his arms. He couldn't stand not touching her anymore. "I know. It's a little overwhelming for me, too." Kissing the top of her head, he breathed in the fruity scent of her shampoo, relished the warmth of her body against his. He had to make this work and convince her he was sincere.

"You can't be serious," she said after a moment or two. Though she didn't pull away, she'd confirmed his fear about her doubting his sincerity. "You have a harem."

"They'll have to be retired, of course." He paused, considered his next statement for about half a second, then figured *what the hell.* "Especially since we'll be getting married. Maybe in the fall. We could double with Allison and Rob."

She stared up at him. "You're crazy."

"I'm The One."

"You can't be."

"Yes, I am. I'm The One. Mr. Right. The man you're destined to spend your life with."

"You can't be," she repeated, still staring at him wide-eyed.

"I can be," he argued, putting some steel into his voice. He wanted Francesca, and he wasn't giving up until he had her. "My new goal is you." Raising his eyebrows, he extended his hand to indicate their surroundings. "And we all know how well my last goal turned out. Wanna make it two for two?"

She pushed out of his arms. "You don't understand. All the women in my family fall in love at first sight. They know instantly when The One walks into their life."

Panic made Tony's hands shake. This wasn't going at all like he'd planned. He was supposed to say *I love you*, then she was supposed to say *I love you, too*, then off into the sunset they'd ride.

And what was this love-at-first-sight nonsense? They'd met in elementary school. How could they have fallen in love back then? He didn't even remember the exact moment they'd first— *Ah ha.* "When did you first see me?" he asked her.

"The first day of fourth grade, I guess."

Double ah ha. Feeling smug, he rocked back on his heels. "So how do you know you didn't fall in love with me right then?"

"Because I just do!" She stormed away from him, turning her back and bracing her hands on one of the wooden tables scattered across the patio. "You can't be The One, Tony," she said quietly, sadly, finally. "I would have known before now."

Tony's heart lurched. This couldn't be happening. "Look at me, *bella*."

With obvious reluctance, she turned.

"Tell me you don't love me. Look me in the eyes and tell me."

Her throat moved as she swallowed. "I don't—" Her lips trembled. Then she spun away from him and ran.

His heart somewhere near his shoes, Tony remained frozen to the spot. *Well, that didn't go very well, did it?*

HOURS LATER, in the cellar beneath the winery, Francesca drew her hand across an oak barrel and fought back tears.

This was one of his favorite places. She felt close to him here. And she needed that closeness at the moment.

Why had she run from him? Why couldn't she grasp his feelings for her?

If she was honest with herself, she'd wanted him for at least the last eleven years, maybe even further back than that. How stupid was it not to rejoice now? Why was she clinging to a stupid family legend? She'd been looking for bells and whistles, but wasn't it possible she'd fallen in love more slowly?

How were you supposed to deal with The One if he came into your life at pre-puberty age?

She'd known he was special, a vital part of her life all along. Had the stories told by her mother and grandmother colored her view of love? Maybe she was different, and the whole love-at-first-sight thing wasn't for her.

As long as this was turning into a truth session, she could admit she was scared about committing to Tony. She'd never considered herself the kind of woman he went for. Yet, he'd been really upset by her breaking off their brief affair. He'd looked as if that was the last thing he wanted. Could he really give up his playboy lifestyle? Could she really be the kind of woman he could love?

She wasn't very fashionable, she certainly wasn't drop-dead gorgeous, and she was a bossy, argumentative workaholic. She had her own opinions and wasn't about to bat her eyes at every word that came out of his mouth.

But he knew all that about her. And still he'd said he loved her.

It was mind-boggling.

And as she examined her own feelings and actions, she couldn't help but relive the nights she'd spent in his arms. They were the most wonderful, precious moments of her life. In the past, she'd imagined them intimately together many times, but the experience had blown away all her fantasies. She'd felt as if she was the only woman in the world—at least the only one for him.

She recalled the night she'd gone to the bar at the Chateau. Her jealousy at finding Tony surrounded by yet another eye-batting harem. His out-of-character protectiveness when she'd asked him how to flirt.

She recalled the wine and cheese party on Saturday. She'd practically told off Pierre von Shalburg because he'd insulted Tony. She had, in effect, sacrificed the resort for him. And nothing was more important to her than the resort and its success.

Nothing except Tony.

Well, damn, she did love him.

She'd probably spent the last nineteen years falling in love with him.

"Ches, I'm not giving up on us," Tony announced as he stalked across the cellar toward her. "I know this has been sudden. I'll give you the time you need, but you're not pushing me away."

Her heart pounding at the realization that he'd found her, Francesca glanced up at him. Their eyes met. She saw his determination, his love...and suddenly it happened.

She just knew.

Her heart recognized him. *The One.*

It wasn't exactly love at first sight. Well, it was. It had just happened in the fourth grade.

Maybe she was a little slow in recognizing the love of her life, but she wasn't about to let a technicality like nearly two decades of friendship stand in her way now.

When he stopped in front of her, she smiled.

"What?" he asked, angling his head.

Slowly, she slid her hands up his chest, absorbing the quick beating of his heart, the warmth of his body. Then she wrapped her arms around his neck. This is where she wanted to be for the rest of her life. She'd known that as she'd woken in his arms this morning. Seeing the love in his eyes now, she had the strength and courage to admit it.

She pressed her lips to his. "I love you."

His hands clenched at her waist; his eyes lit with surprise. "You do?"

"Oh, yeah."

"How much?"

She trailed her fingers through his hair. "How about I show you?"

"When?"

"How about now?"

He smiled, then pulled her close, his cheek sliding against hers. "Now's good for me."

Epilogue

"CHES, let's go, we're going to be late."

Francesca glared at herself in the mirror. "I can't get this stupid veil straight."

From the other side of the suite's door, Tony asked, "Isn't your mom supposed to be helping?"

"She ran out crying again."

"Good grief." Seconds later, the door swung open. Tony, clad in a perfectly-tailored black tuxedo, stood in the opening.

Francesca gasped and held up her hands—though she did manage a quick glimpse. Her eyes boggled at the incredibly sexy sight of him. "Out! It's bad luck to see me before the wedding."

Smiling widely, he crossed to her. "We don't need luck."

Leave it to Tony to flout convention. It was one of the things she loved most about him.

His deep-brown eyes focused on her face, and he grasped her hand, placing a warm kiss on her palm. "You're the most beautiful woman in the world."

Flushing, she let her gaze slide over him as well. Combed-back glossy black hair, broad shoulders, crisp white shirt, black slacks. *Wow.* "You'll do."

Laughing, he pulled her into his arms.

She sighed against him, inhaling the familiar scent of

his cologne, and her veil flopped to one side again. She clamped her hand over the flimsy thing. "What are we going to do about this?"

He reached his hand into his coat pocket. "I think this will come in handy."

Pulling out an elegant rhinestone tiara—at least she assumed those sparkling gems were rhinestones, one never knew with Tony—he yanked out the pins holding her veil on her head and set the crown on top instead. After a thorough once over, he turned her to face the mirror. "My exquisite bride."

Francesca hardly knew the woman staring back at her in snow-white satin and tulle. The tiara added just a bit of sparkle. Tony had made everything perfect, as usual.

"Every Prince of the Universe has to have a princess."

In the mirror, she cut her gaze to his. "I only called you that aloud once—and only after you balked at crawling on the floor of the restaurant to find Mrs. Grimsley's diamond earring."

He looked shocked. "I thought it was a compliment."

She smiled and leaned back against him. As his arms slid around her, she thought about the whirlwind of the last seven months—a steady run of bookings, parties, planning, strategizing, and falling deeper in love as each day passed. The only drawback had been the distinct level of hostility she'd felt from the female population trolling through their resort when they found out the charming and gorgeous Tony Galini was definitely not available.

Okay, so maybe that wasn't a drawback.

Pierre von—whoops, make that Hoyt Ewing had been back three times to visit and had given Tony permission to tell Francesca his secret. For the sake of his reputation, they kept up the pretense of his snobby critic persona. And, really, the staff hadn't suffered too much. Only rolling her eyes once or twice, Mabel supplied him with an extra stack of *extra*-white and fluffy towels each morning. Derrick had learned to swallow his nervousness with important guests and Hoyt didn't try to change any more of Chef Carlos's recipes.

Not wanting to share the spotlight, Tony had decided against a double wedding with Allison and Rob, who'd finally jumped into happily-ever-after at the beginning of September. So, here they were, three days before Christmas, ready to take the plunge themselves.

Sometimes Francesca still couldn't believe how lucky she was.

He spun her in his arms, his eyes suddenly serious and intent as his gaze searched her face. "I love you."

Her stomach fluttered. She twined her arms around his neck. "I love you."

His mouth descended on hers, and when their lips touched she felt the familiar but somehow never expected thrill race through her blood. After all the preparations and parties, she couldn't wait to have him all to herself. Forever.

A knock on the door interrupted their kiss—no doubt their last one as bachelor and bachelorette.

Reluctantly, Francesca pulled back, even as she heard Hoyt's voice. "Let's go, bubba."

She shook her head. "I can't believe you asked him to be best man."

"Excuse me, Just-About-To-Be Mrs. Galini, *I'm* the best man. Don't you forget it."

Hooking her arm around his, Francesca walked beside him toward the door and their future. "I'm sure you'll keep reminding me."

Tony swung her into his arms, kissing her lightly on the lips. "Count on it, *bella*. For at least the next fifty years or so."

HARLEQUIN
Temptation

THE WRONG BED

What happens when a girl finds herself in the *wrong* bed…with the *right* guy?

Find out in:

#866 NAUGHTY BY NATURE by Jule McBride
February 2002

#870 SOMETHING WILD by Toni Blake
March 2002

#874 CARRIED AWAY by Donna Kauffman
April 2002

#878 HER PERFECT STRANGER by Jill Shalvis
May 2002

#882 BARELY MISTAKEN by Jennifer LaBrecque
June 2002

#886 TWO TO TANGLE by Leslie Kelly
July 2002

Midnight mix-ups have never been so much fun!

HARLEQUIN®
Makes any time special ®

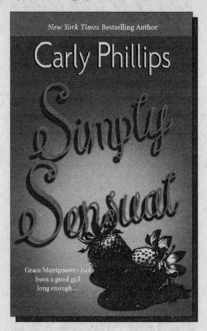
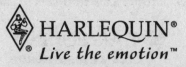

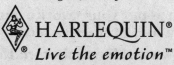

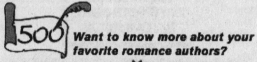

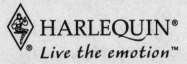

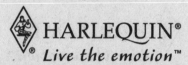